Death's

There were four humps un[der] [the] fire. Two of them snored lou[dly.] [Slocum] drew his Colt, and squatted by the first sleeper. He stuck a finger to the man's lips and put the gun muzzle in his face.

"Get up slow. No tricks. No sound," Slocum whispered.

The man obeyed and rose with his arms high. With him in view, Slocum did the same to the next one. He clapped his left hand over the man's protest.

"Shut up," Slocum hissed, and the wide-eyed man obeyed.

"Huh?" the next one grunted, sitting up.

"Shut up. Get out here." Slocum saw him move under the covers and knew he had a pistol.

The .44 in Slocum's fist sent an orange flare out of the muzzle and made an ear-shattering blast. The man's shot was muffled by the blankets, and he fell back from the lead that struck his face like a thud on a watermelon.

DON'T MISS THESE
ALL-ACTION WESTERN SERIES
FROM THE BERKLEY PUBLISHING GROUP

JAKE LOGAN

SLOCUM
AND PEARL
OF THE RIO GRANDE

JOVE BOOKS, NEW YORK

THE BERKLEY PUBLISHING GROUP
Published by the Penguin Group
Penguin Group (USA) Inc.
375 Hudson Street, New York, New York 10014, USA
Penguin Group (Canada), 90 Eglinton Avenue East, Suite 700, Toronto, Ontario M4P 2Y3, Canada
(a division of Pearson Penguin Canada Inc.)
Penguin Books Ltd., 80 Strand, London WC2R 0RL, England
Penguin Group Ireland, 25 St. Stephen's Green, Dublin 2, Ireland (a division of Penguin Books Ltd.)
Penguin Group (Australia), 250 Camberwell Road, Camberwell, Victoria 3124, Australia
(a division of Pearson Australia Group Pty. Ltd.)
Penguin Books India Pvt. Ltd., 11 Community Centre, Panchsheel Park, New Delhi—110 017, India
Penguin Group (NZ), 67 Apollo Drive, Rosedale, North Shore 0632, New Zealand
(a division of Pearson New Zealand Ltd.)
Penguin Books (South Africa) (Pty.) Ltd., 24 Sturdee Avenue, Rosebank, Johannesburg 2196,
South Africa

Penguin Books Ltd., Registered Offices: 80 Strand, London WC2R 0RL, England

This is a work of fiction. Names, characters, places, and incidents either are the product of the author's imagination or are used fictitiously, and any resemblance to actual persons, living or dead, business establishments, events, or locales is entirely coincidental.

SLOCUM AND PEARL OF THE RIO GRANDE

A Jove Book / published by arrangement with the author

PRINTING HISTORY
Jove edition / October 2008

ISBN: 978-0-515-14539-7

JOVE®
Jove Books are published by The Berkley Publishing Group,
a division of Penguin Group (USA) Inc.,
375 Hudson Street, New York, New York 10014.
JOVE is a registered trademark of Penguin Group (USA) Inc.
The "J" design is a trademark belonging to Penguin Group (USA) Inc.

PRINTED IN THE UNITED STATES OF AMERICA

10 9 8 7 6 5 4 3 2 1

1

The bank of the towering dry wash jutted out and forced him to rein the buckskin around the abutment. He'd kept to the confines of the deep arroyos since he'd come off the mountains from over on the Pecos—out of sight, out of mind. The long slopes he rode through eventually dumped into the Rio Grande. This high up in New Mexico, the land was studded with junipers. At a lower elevation there was lots of open country to spot a rider in. One thing that folks noticed and even gossiped about was a stranger riding through their land. He didn't need anyone talking about where he was headed.

Far to the north of him, the Rockies started in Colorado. From a high point, he could see the snowy peaks on a clear day. To the south, he could ride into Santa Fe in a day or so. The notion of Santa Fe made his mouth water for some fine food and good liquor. There'd be some of both to be found around the plaza—after dark in one of the cantinas facing the park, there'd be a sloe-eyed señorita to dance with him. And come daylight, he'd find her asleep in his warm bed, worn out from his excessive lovemaking the night before.

They were all lovely—the women of Santa Fe. But he had no plans to visit the territorial capital this time; he intended to take the old Spanish Trail up through Colorado and Utah, then end up in California or hell knows where.

It was the loud squeaking of a *carreta*'s greaseless axle that caught his attention. He must be nearing the Taos Road. He could visualize the two-wheeled vehicle loaded down with supplies, powered by two oxen, with a Mexican man in sandals and white clothing and with a whip in his hand plodding along beside them.

Slocum discovered a cut in the sidewall of the wash, and sent the tough mountain pony to the top of the bank for a look-see. The buckskin gelding he called Heck lunged up the steep slope in hard cat-hops to gain the brim. On the flat ground, Slocum reined him in between two large junipers for cover and dug the brass telescope out of his saddlebags.

The scope tubes extended, he looked through the eyepiece. Instead of a *carreta,* he saw a dancing barb horse with its dish face, alert pin ears, and smoky gray color. Then he could see the rider and frowned. For a second, he thought the straight-backed rider was a youth, a boy. But no, it was a lady under the flat-crowned hat. She wore a thick leather coat lined with wool. Her throat was wrapped in a white silk rag with blue polka dots, and her black hair was in long, tight braids that danced below her shoulders.

How old was she? No telling, but from her fine horse to her silver earrings that glinted in the bright sun, something about her attracted him. Then the *carreta* came into sight, and he smiled at the load it bore. A young Hereford bull rode inside the pole enclosure, and even at the distance, his red and white coat glistened. The sire's husky bawling carried to where Slocum sat Heck high above the road in the clump of junipers. From the fancy bull to the woman's light-footed horse, everything spelled money, but what he could see of her face fascinated him more than anything else.

The north wind had cut into him ever since he'd left the dry wash's protection, and he buttoned his unlined jumper against it. He was curious about the woman aboard the gray stud as he let his own mount catch his breath. But there was no way for him to meet her. Besides, he needed to move on. There was no telling where those two deputies from Kansas were. He hoped he'd left them at Fort Union stumped about his whereabouts.

He ran his tongue over his teeth. There was a story about

that fine bull and the young woman that he'd like to hear. Rich Hispanic families did not let unwed girls go about on horseback unchaperoned with bull haulers.

He shrugged and put away the scope. It was time to take the road. He gathered his reins to draw Heck's head up. The mountain pony was busy snatching mouthfuls of dry grass. A horse like that never missed a chance to eat—a trait that made his kind easy keepers.

Slocum's thoughts were still on the lady, her gray horse, and the bull as he booted Heck for the road. Maybe when he passed them on his way, he'd learn more about her. In a short while, he overtook the small entourage and removed his hat for her. The squeal of the axle was distracting, but over it he said "Good morning" in Spanish.

She nodded, but her dark eyes did not meet his. Her lips remained in a tight line and her attention was focused on the hills ahead.

"Nice bull," he said.

She agreed with a sharp nod and checked the dancing stallion. A gust of wind forced her to turn her head aside, and when the wind subsided, she faced the front again. Her coffee-cream coloration was complemented by her black eyebrows and long black eyelashes. Riding along beside her, he wished he could look into her dark eyes. She was in her early twenties, even younger than he'd first thought.

Since she was double-wrapped in the silk scarf, she had no visible neck, but he could imagine it. Obviously, she was not allowing him to enter her world. Someone's wife? Or simply a strong-willed young woman who wanted no part of a cowboy who looked like he was riding the chuck line?

Moistening his lips, he realized that his beard stubble didn't help his appearance either.

"May I ask your name?" He didn't expect an answer. Although they were only a few feet apart, he felt miles away from her.

"Perla. Perla Peralta."

"Pearl." He said the translation of her name and nodded in gratitude for her introduction. "Slocum is mine."

If she heard him over the bull's bellowing and the cart's protests, she never batted an eye until she turned and met his gaze. "You live nearby here?"

He shook his head.

"I will need a place to stable him this afternoon." She meant her bull.

"I'm riding on. Can I find you a place in the next village?"

"There is a church there. Perhaps the padre will know of a place." Her words sounded more like an internal conversation than one she was sharing with him.

He nodded. "Perhaps we shall meet again, Señorita Peralta."

"Señora."

"Señora."

Someone's wife? Strange indeed that a man would allow his lovely young wife, without protection, to bring home such a high-priced bull on a notorious road known for robberies and murders. He saluted her and put Heck in a short lope. He'd better get Perla off his mind. He would never penetrate the invisible shield around her. Simply meeting Señora Peralta had roiled his guts, and the short conversation had only made him that much more eager to reach her.

Pearl of the Rio Grande. He wanted to laugh. He'd never heard of anyone finding a pearl in that river, but maybe he had seen the real thing in their brief meeting. And already he'd lost her. She'd evaporated from his life like a small mud hole from a summer shower would evaporate overnight in this arid land.

Still, the straight-backed rider on the dancing gray stallion wasn't really gone—he couldn't forget her.

2

The mission at San Juan was a small chapel. Stinging grit from the the wind forced him to duck his head to save his hat. He felt grateful to see the large black letters on the side of the building across the street—CANTINA. With Heck hitched at the rack and the structure blocking some of the wind from the buckskin, Slocum went inside the left double door. The batwing doors were tied back for the cold weather. He found the interior dark save for some flickering candle lamps.

A mustached bartender nodded, wiping the bar with a rag as if waiting for his order. *"Buenos dias, hombre."*

"Same to you." Satisfied they were the only ones in the place, Slocum crossed to the dark bar.

"What can I do for you?" the bartender asked.

"A bottle of whiskey and a glass."

"Sí." The man was in his forties, thickly built but not tall. He dropped to his knees and checked his supply under the back bar. "You must be from the road."

"Yes. I'll need a place to stay tonight." He rested his hands on the rounded edge of the bar and stretched his stiff back muscles.

Movement to his right made him glance at the short woman who peered with dark eyes at him, half obscured by the curtain hung over the hall doorway. She smiled and nodded, then frowned at the barkeep, who was still kneeling down searching.

"I thought he was praying," she said, and laughed. Her hair was short and her dark eyes as large as a doe's. Her thick lower lip was too large and her exposed cleavage looked like two tubes above the rim of the thin blouse. She whirled around like a free spirit showing off her shapely calves, and then joined him at the bar.

She looked him up and down. "You are a *grande hombre*."

"Slocum."

"Ah, my name is Casita. What is Arturo doing back there?" She stood on her toes to try to see the barkeep, and still was too short.

Ah, is Kentucky Gold good enough?" Arturo asked at last.

Slocum nodded. "You drink whiskey?" he asked Casita.

"Sure," she said, acting as if the offer was special to her.

"Make it two glasses." Slocum dug in his pocket to pay.

Arturo nodded and set another glass on the bar. "Three pesos."

Slocum put the money on the bar top and nodded to the man. With Casita clinging to his waist and driving a breast into his hip, they went to a rear table. She slid in the bench against the wall, and held out her hand for a match to light the candle stuck in the neck of a liquor bottle. He set down the whiskey and found her one. On her knees atop the bench, she struck the torpedo-head match and it flared, igniting the wick. With a smile for her, Slocum slipped onto the bench beside her, and cut the seal of the whiskey bottle with his jackknife. She smoothed her skirt and sat back down with her hip pressed against him.

"I can see you are a man who likes his whiskey," she said.

He nodded. "Cuts the trail dust."

"Do you need to leave before morning?"

He shook his head and pulled the cork, then splashed some whiskey in each glass. "I'm in no big rush. Here's to our health."

She clinked her glass to his. Then she kissed him hard on the mouth to seal the deal.

"Here's to good health," she repeated, and met his gaze. "And much fun."

"Much fun."

Three men entered, and she twisted around to look at them. A big gringo led two young vaqueros into the room. At the sight of them, she slipped down in her seat like she wanted to shrivel up.

"Where's Maria?" the big man demanded of Arturo. He looked around like an angry bear, and must not have seen them before he turned back to the barman.

"She is not here, Señor."

"Where in the fuck is she?"

Arturo shrugged. "Maybe she went to Española."

"You're hiding her. Gawdamnit."

"No, Señor. She is not here."

Then the man turned in the direction of Slocum and Casita. He stalked across the room toward them. Angry intent was written in his dark eyes and a tic in his cheek showed his internal rage.

At the sight of him, Slocum slapped the cork down in the bottle and started to slide out to stand. This guy had troubles, but he might get himself a lot more charging at Slocum like that.

"He's a mean man," Casita whispered, and Slocum acknowledged her words but never glanced at her.

"Who're you?" the bully demanded.

"Slocum," he said, looking hard at the man, satisfied the two young riders were drinking *cerveza* at the bar and only watching the man's tirade.

"What're you doing in this country?" he demanded.

"You the damn law?"

"You stay here, you'll learn who I am." He pushed in close like he was going to get in Slocum's face.

His eyes flew wide open when Slocum's .44 muzzle jabbed him in the gut. He started to back away, and Slocum followed him keeping the gun pressed hard into his belly. "Don't mistake me, I'll blow daylight through you. What's your name?"

"Harvey Ryan, Harvey Ryan."

"Well, Slocum's mine, Harvey Ryan. Next time you want to

run over me, you'd better be prepared to die. 'Cause I'll send you to hell."

"All right, you made your point. All right—"

"You don't know points. But you'd damn sure better learn them and quick."

Slocum shoved him backward with his free hand and holstered his Colt. "Now get the hell out of here and don't come back."

"Who—" Ryan held his hands out to ward Slocum off. "I'm leaving."

"Good." Slocum watched the two vaqueros fade out the door, and Ryan followed them.

He paused at the door. "Slocum, you ain't heard the last of this."

"They got a newspaper here?" Slocum asked.

"Why?"

"You better have your funeral notice written up if you ever try to charge me again."

Whatever Ryan said under his breath while going out the door, Slocum couldn't understand.

"He is a very bad hombre," Casita said, looking concerned.

Arturo came to the end of the bar. "He's a big bully. *Gracias, hombre.*"

Slocum raised his glass of whiskey to the man. "May he fall down and break his leg."

"Ah, that would be good for him," Casita said, scooting close to Slocum again. "Poor Maria had to leave here last night, she feared him so much."

"Is there no law here?"

"No," she said. "The sheriff is on his payroll."

Arturo nodded.

"Sounds to me like you folks have real problems."

She rose and squeezed his head between her palms to kiss him on the cheek. "Forget that *bastardo*. You and me, we have fun, no?"

He put both hands on her slender hips. Their mouths met, and he imagined her short body under the thin clothing. Ah, Hispanic women often had few inhibitions.

They drank his whiskey and slipped into a relaxed state. She spoke about her mother in Chihuahua and about the man she came up to San Juan to marry, how he had become ill and died before they could be blessed by the padre. Slocum figured that part was a fabrication that she used to justify being a *puta*.

Soon, she was on her knees on top of the bench beside him, pressing her boobs into his arm and kissing him on the face and lips like a woman hungry for him or hungry for his attentions. Her small hands were like butterfly wings flitting over a plant. He was enjoying the attention, and the whiskey was releasing the tension of the past days.

"Are you hungry?" she whispered, cupping her hand on his ear.

"For what?" He blinked at her.

"Food?"

"No."

"Good," she said, scooting off the bench. "Let's go to my room."

"Can we drink back there?" he asked.

As if caught off guard, she started to blush. "Sure."

Bottle and glasses in his hand, he unlimbered off the bench and, with Casita attached to his waist, started for the curtain door.

The front door slammed open, and he turned back to see Perla standing in the shadowy light of the cantina. She blinked, then went to the bar and spoke to Arturo.

"Who is she?" Casita whispered to Slocum with a frown of suspicion.

"Señora Peralta."

"What does she want in here?" Casita whispered.

"Señor," the bartender called to Slocum. "This lady wishes to hire a guard. I told her about you."

He handed Casita the whiskey bottle and glasses, excused himself, then removed his hat. "Ah, Señora Peralta, good day."

"Señor. Oh, you are the man from the road?"

"Yes."

"I would like to hire someone to guard the prize bull King Arthur."

"For how long?"

"How long would you like to work?"

Forever for you. "I mean, tonight or longer?"

"The ranch is several days north of Española." Her dark eyes looked hard at him like she expected him to open up to her.

"Why hire a guard now?"

"I don't want anything to happen to him. He is a very expensive bull."

"You think the road beyond here is more dangerous?"

"Yes, or I would have hired a guard sooner."

"What do you pay?"

She nodded, looking as if she was about to dicker on the wages. "Thirty dollars to get me to the ranch."

"Pay me fifty and I'm your man."

"How do I know you can do it?"

"Oh, he can do it," Casita said. "He will be with you in one hour."

Perla swept off her flat-crowned hat and looked angrily at her. "Why?"

Hands on her hips, feet apart, Casita glared at Perla. " 'Cause he is mine for one hour."

Perla looked at the ceiling for help and tapped her hard boot sole on the packed dirt floor before she turned away for the door. Stopping, she spun around and cut a hard glace at Casita. "One hour is all you get. Then send him to me at the stables."

"Gracias, señora." Casita bowed to her.

Slocum gave Perla a hard nod of approval and she left.

"Ah, cowboy, now you have work, no?"

"And so do you." He laughed aloud and caught Casita's arm in his elbow.

Halfway down the narrow hallway with her, Slocum could smell woman's musk and cheap perfume. She showed him into her small room, which contained a bed, a chair, and a cross on the wall. Under it on a shelf, two candles in red glassware flickered. A black Sunday dress hung on the opposite wall. All of her earthly goods.

She placed the whiskey and glasses on the small stand with the mirror. He began to toe off his boots, and she started to unbutton his shirt. Her small fingers worked swiftly as he undid his gun belt and hung it on the ladder-back chair.

"Do you know that woman?" he asked.

She smiled up from undressing him. "They own a large ranch."

That didn't make sense to him. Why was a big rancher hiring a guard at the last minute? There was something there he'd have to learn all about. When his shirt was open, she kissed the trace of hair that ran down his middle over his flat belly. He undid his pants, and let them fall to his ankles as her mouth moved lower.

Her short fingers closed around his shaft, pulling gently on it, and her lips began to nibble at the head. He clutched her ears. His fingers were busy teasing them. As his erection rose, she became caught up on in her own enthusiasm and took on more of the shaft. The hard roof of her mouth scoured the head while she sucked hard on it—in and out.

Finally, he pulled her to her feet. Bleary-eyed and gasping for breath, she stripped her blouse off over her head. Then she wiggled out of her skirt, the red light of the candles reflecting off her cocoa skin as she stepped free of it. He fondled her small breasts and bent over to kiss her. She locked her arms around his neck, and her hungry mouth locked on his. Her tongue tasted salty.

They floated to the bed in one fluid motion. With her legs wide apart for his entry, she pulled him down on top of her. His erection slid through her gates with a soft "Oh" that escaped from her mouth. He probed her in short strokes while his hips ached to pound her to the very depths.

With her legs stuck in the air, her back was arched to accept him. He soon was bumping against her pubic bone, and the stiff hair was rubbing hard between them with each plunge in and out. His breath raged through his throat like a fiery torch, and his heart beat in double time, his back and butt driving with each rise and fall and his balls slapping her butt.

Like a clamp being screwed down, her contracting walls soon made each drive harder and harder for him. It strained the tight skin on the throbbing head, until at last he felt the volcanic force rise from deep in his scrotum. Two red-hot needles speared the halves of his butt—then, buried to the hilt, he came.

The world spun him dizzy and his strength flew away like a released quail. Stiff-armed over her, he savored the moment as he looked down at her compact sensuous body.

"*Gracias,* Casita."

She pulled him back down and kissed him, squirming her lithe form underneath him. "Ah, you can't leave me yet, hombre."

He nodded numbly. "I was only getting my breath."

A smile crossed her face, half hidden by her disheveled hair. "*Sí,* we have much more to do. That rich bitch will just have to wait. Besides, I bet she is cold as ice in bed."

Slocum winked at her. Perla would not be a Casita. Oh, well, he'd probably never find that out.

3

An hour later, going out of the cantina's front door, he turned up the collar of his jumper against the gusts of wind laden with stinging grit and dust. He undid the reins wrapped around the rack and led Heck up the street to the stables. In half a block, he saw the *carreta* in front of the building marked LIVERY. With his hard calloused palm, he wiped his mouth, and considered the past hour of pleasure in the arms of Casita. It was time for him to go to work for the lovely señora and protect her prize white-faced bull.

He fought the large door open against the wind, and at last led Heck inside the stables. In the shadowy darkness of the building, he reset the door, grateful to escape the biting wind. He turned and saw someone bringing a candle lamp.

"So you have arrived," Perla said with an edge to her voice.

"Yes," he said, and began to undo his latigos on the saddle. With the girth undone, he lifted the saddle and pads off the buckskin and turned to face her with his hands full. "I guess there is a rack for this?"

"Yes." She blinked as if taken aback, then reached out and took the bridle reins. "Follow me."

I'd follow you to the end of the earth. He fell in behind Heck as she led them through the cobwebbed interior to where the bull was contained in a pole-sided stall. Their shadows

13

from the lamplight danced on the walls and hay. The two oxen were tied at a rack by ropes from their nose rings, and were munching on the hay in front of them. He could hear the nearby snort and pawing of the gray stallion in an enclosed box stall as Perla showed him to a tie stall for Heck.

"This should be satisfactory?" she asked.

"Mighty fine. What time do we leave in the morning?" He nodded to the padre who was coming down the center aisle toward them.

"Oh, Father Malloy, I shall be right there," she said, and turned back to Slocum.

"Very well, Señora," said the priest.

She spoke to Slocum. "I would think we should be on the road by daylight?"

"You're the boss. Where is the ox driver? Will I need to check on him?"

"Perhaps. His name is Diego Santiago. He is asleep in the office. I am staying at the rectory this evening." She handed him the lamp and seemed ready to leave with the padre.

Slocum nodded. "Diego and I will be ready. One more thing before you leave."

"Yes?"

"Do you know of anyone who wants this bull or you bad enough to take either one of you by force?"

She shook her head. "There are many evil men in this world."

"I mean you specifically."

"No one in particular."

"Fine. Have a good evening." He touched his hat brim for her.

"Thanks, Father," she said to the priest. "I am certain I could have walked to the rectory by myself."

"No, Señora, I wanted to escort you personally."

"That's very kind . . ." The sound of her voice trailed off as Slocum watched the two disappear in the building's darkness and considered finding himself an evening meal. Where was her *carreta* man? He'd better look for him. The lantern in his hand, he went toward the front, finding the office empty save for the sleeping driver.

"You want some food?" he asked, shaking the man awake.

"What?"

Slocum smiled at the man's surprised face. "I am her new guard. You want supper?"

"*Sí.*"

"My name's Slocum."

"Diego, Diego Santiago."

"I got that. You know a place we can get some food?"

"There is a woman—"

Slocum shook his head. "I'll buy. Is there a place serves good food?"

"There is a café, but I never eat there. It costs too much."

"I'm buying. Come, we eat at the café."

"But I am not dressed—"

"If you have the money, dress is unimportant. Come on, we need to be up and loaded by daybreak."

"*Sí,* she is in a big hurry this time."

After he blew out the candle lamp, he glanced over at the man. "How often do you do this?"

"Other times it was furniture, and once two new doors for the hacienda."

"You and her went for them?"

"*Sí.*"

"What about the *patrón*? What does he do when she is gone?"

"Oh, the *patrón* has been dead for three years. *Bandidos* shot him when they raided the ranch."

"I see." So there was no señor alive. That was interesting, too. "Let's get some food. You can tell me about the raid."

"It was a very bad time . . ."

Slocum heard about the band of masked outlaws that swept down and killed the *patrón* and even children. Over the supper of fire-roasted *cabrito,* he learned how they had raided the ranch, raped the women and even young girls, forced the *patrón* to open the safe, then shot him and taken the money, Perla's jewelry, and many good horses when they fled.

"Who were they?"

"We never knew. They all wore masks. The law made WANTED posters for them, but none were ever arrested and I don't know who they are. It has been very hard for the señora. All the money was stolen and the best workers were shot, or they quit in fear the *bandidos* would come back again."

Slocum'd heard there were outlaws all over the land. He looked up from the forkful of tender goat and met the man's sad gaze. "Did they rape her?"

Diego swallowed hard and nodded. "It was a bad day. The worst one in my life."

"I can bet it was. *Gracias* for telling me. I know it was hard to do that."

Slowly chewing the tender meat, he realized why she had such a distant air about her. It was her reaction to the tragedy. Yet she still had to run the ranch. Damn, some folks were dealt a hard hand in their lives.

4

Overnight, the wind died down, but a light frost touched things. His breath made vapor clouds, and he wished for a thick wool-lined leather coat instead of the unlined jumper. He'd undo his sleeping blanket for an overcoat once they were on their way. Her gray was curried, saddled, and ready. Heck was set also.

Diego led the white-faced bull out of the barn to the hitched *carreta,* parked in a depression so the rear end was close to the ground and the bull could step up into it. The young stud was frisky in the cool air. He wanted to run and play, but the man held him back by bracing his sandals and waiting for his fool-ishness to end. At last, with the soft purple light spreading over the land, the bull went into the wagon—he was obviously well trained—and Diego hitched him.

Slocum and Diego squatted and chewed on hard pepper jerky. When Slocum looked up, he saw Perla coming. She wore leather leggings under her divided skirt and the polka-dot scarf around her throat. Her spurs clinked like little bells in the morning's silence.

"Good morning," she said, and went to unhitch her gray. Leading him over, she nodded to Slocum and Diego. "I am ready."

When Slocum moved toward her to help her mount, she shook her head. "I can get on my own horse. Thank you."

17

He rubbed his calloused hand over his whisker-bristled mouth. She still had her armor. It was intact. Even looking as grubby as he did, he could usually break through. But not this morning anyway. He mounted Heck for the day's slow journey, and the noisy wagon began to creak away, the young bull shifting around to brace himself against a fall.

Diego and his oxen trudged along headed for the road. The village sat a good quarter mile from the Taos Road, as if it had no desire to be part of its activity. Women stared at them from the doorways of their jacales, protectively keeping small children behind them.

Two fighting cocks flew at each other in the center of the road, ignoring the oncoming entourage, busy in a flutter of bright feathers flying at each other for male seniority. When Perla drew close on the gray, they fled to restart their sparring again on the bare ground of a yard.

A burro brayed and some goats answered, sounding impatient to be milked or fed. Slocum had unfurled his blanket and huddled under it seeking warmth, keeping an eye out for any sign of trouble. He jabbed Heck into a lope to move up beside her.

"I will go ahead and check out anything I see."

She nodded in approval. "I think if we have trouble, it will be above Española."

"You have enemies there?"

She gave a small shrug as if that made no difference. "It is a bad world we live in."

"I agree. I will ride on and survey the road ahead for trouble."

"Yes." Her approval matched the sharp wind—cold.

He sent Heck off in a short lope. The road skirted the fields where dry corn fodder was shucked. The golden leaves of the cottonwoods' fall foliage had begun to fade. Winter would not be far away. How had he forgotten so soon those promises to himself—to spend winters in San Antonio, where the brown-skinned women hat-danced in the warm sun around the Alamo square. Where winter could be spent leisurely and with little chill.

Up here, a dry country surrounded them. It was a land of greasewood and cactus that had survived the centuries with little rain. Not huge spiny cactus plants, but low-growing beds of prickly pear and cholla, with some mesquite, greasewood, and brown bunchgrass that was like stiff straw.

He found little but freighters on the road and some pack trains of burros loaded with firewood. Dry sticks scrounged off the desert floor made small hot cooking fires. He pulled the blanket tighter, reminded of the cold penetrating his bones. A fiery blaze would go good at that moment for him.

At Arroyo Seco, a small huddle of jacales and small stores, he found a cantina and stopped for a drink and information. The interior was dark and reeked of fermented pulque, a homemade corn product like beer.

"Ah, Señor?" the short man with the tight twisted mustache said from behind the bar.

"Whiskey? Mescal?"

The man nodded and set a bottle and glass on the scarred surface. "You are passing through?"

"Yes, on the road." He poured himself some in a glass and looked around the room.

A few locals drank pulque in one corner and argued about something inaudibly. Slocum turned back, he would learn little in this sour stinking dive. Perhaps he would try to find a place for his party to stop near here. He downed the cheap whiskey in three tries. It cut the dust and he set the glass down. *"Gracias."*

The barkeep recorked the bottle, looked at the amount left, and said half a dollar. Slocum paid him, then went back out into the sunshine. It was still cold, but the sun did provide some heat. In the saddle, he rode on down through the community. He found a blacksmith working in his shop, which smelled of burning coal, and stopped to talk to him.

The smithy was drawing out iron, heating rods and beating them flat on the anvil for straps. He looked up and spoke in Spanish. "Good afternoon. May I help you?"

"I am looking for a place to rest tonight. I have a purebred bull in a *carreta*."

"There is a stable here." He motioned to the adjoining shed.

"Good. Is there a place for a señora to stay tonight?"

"Your wife?"

Slocum shook his head. "No, my *patrón*."

"There is a widow woman on the hill would board her."

"Thanks, I will see you this evening."

The man nodded and resumed his loud ringing pounding.

Slocum found a woman in the street to make him some bean-and-meat burritos, and he carried them back for he knew Perla had no provisions. It was near noontime by the sun, and he short-loped Heck on his way to meet them.

This bull hauling was going to be boring with Perla's cold shoulder and the slow movement of the *carreta*—what had made him take the job anyway? He passed some more freighters in his journey. With long strings of oxen and double wagons, they were headed north with loads.

He found her coming up the road and set Heck down in front of her. "I bought you some food and there is a stable in Arroyo Seco. And a widow would put you up there."

She nodded and took the burrito, which was wrapped in a newspaper, from him. "I guess we can stop there."

"I'll tell Diego."

She unwrapped the burrito and nodded. "I will pay you for this."

He waved her off and started for Diego and the cart, which was trailing her by a hundred feet.

"Wait," she said. "My enemies are beyond Española. They are a band of men who push people around."

"Who are they?"

"The Booster brothers."

He nodded. That name came from somewhere in his trail-driving days. Maybe he knew them.

Her eyes narrowed. "You know them?"

"Not really."

Her gaze moved away. "Do you know them?"

"No, ma'am, but if they mess with you, they better have their life insurance paid in full."

She snickered. "They are mean men. They know I am alone now. I could not afford enough full-time pistoleros to ward them off. Then I began to worry as I came north, what if they tried to steal King Arthur?"

"I'm here, there is no need to worry."

"Do you know anything about them?"

"No. But let me feed Diego and then you can tell me everything. I am anxious to hear about them."

"Yes. Do that."

The urgent sound in her voice told him enough. There was something else here besides the story Diego had told him the night before. The driver of the *carreta* looked pleased at Slocum's offering and thanked him for the food. King Arthur bellowed at them and shook his large white horns.

He would get his food late in the afternoon.

Slocum rode ahead, anxious to hear what Perla had to say. He checked around, saw nothing out of place, reset the six-gun on his hip, and reined in beside her.

"Tell me about the gang that killed your husband." With a nod of approval, she began her story between small bites of food.

"They all wore masks. They came to the ranch in the night—three years ago. They shot my husband. There were six or seven of them. They robbed the safe of all our money. Took my jewelry. Killed men, women, and children—" Underneath the leather coat, her shoulders shook in revulsion, and she closed her eyes, swallowing hard.

"I know they will come back—again. The law can't find them or does not want to. They must know I have made some money from selling cattle. Last night I couldn't tell you this—I didn't know you. But when you were ready exactly at dawn as I asked, I knew then you were more than a guard."

"These Boosters. They are not the same gang?"

She shook her head quickly. "No, no, the killers all wore masks. We didn't know them. The Boosters charge us for protection."

He nodded, though he had his doubts. "How far away is your ranch?"

"Four or five days' ride at this speed. I forgot how slow the *carreta* traveled." She looked embarrassed.

"No problem. We'll be watchful, and first I want to get your new sire home safely. Then perhaps we can do something about the brothers."

"I didn't ask you to come and get killed for me."

"I don't aim to let that happen." He touched his hat brim and pulled aside so she would eat. Their closeness on horseback had obviously made her uneasy. "One thing at a time."

"Slocum, I can't afford a large force of gunmen."

"Down in Texas, they would send a Ranger. One bunch of outlaws, one Ranger."

"Were you a Ranger?" She frowned at him.

"No, ma'am. But I can act like I am."

She paused, as if digesting his words, then nodded slowly. "Yes, I believe you could."

Their stay overnight at Arroyo Seco went well, and early the next morning they were headed for Española. Slocum rode ahead to make arrangements for her to stay with a merchant and his wife there who she'd dealt with before. He found the town was little more than scattered adobe hovels with a few stores and cantinas—plus a church.

Slocum met the rotund merchant, Mr. Goldfarb, in his store, and the man was pleased she had hired a man to help her make the trip.

"Señora Peralta is such a wonderful lady and her husband was a fine man—oh, I was shocked when I learned of the raid and his murder," said Goldfarb.

"What did the law do about it?"

"Not much besides print posters. Oh, the posse rode after them, but they lost their tracks."

"This gang is still robbing and stealing?"

"Who knows? There are so many desperadoes in this territory."

"Do they operate out of the north?"

The man turned up his palms. "I don't know."

"Thanks. The señora and the *carreta* will be here in mid-afternoon."

"I will have my man help them."

"She would appreciate that."

"Oh, anything she needs."

Slocum thanked him and left the store. He noted a cowboy under a wide-brimmed felt hat sitting on a nail keg with his large knife, whittling. With each stroke, he was making long shavings, and he spoke in a Texas drawl. "That you, Slocum?"

"Who's asking?" He blinked at the man, who needed a shave.

"Collie Bill Hankins." He used the stick to shove the hat back on his shoulders, revealing the sun-dark face and snowy forehead of a man in his thirties. He smiled. "Thought it was you when I seen you ride in a spell ago."

"What've you been doing up here?"

"Drifting. You working?" Collie Bill dropped back to his whittling.

"Some. Are you?"

Collie Bill shook his head. "I was going over to Cimarron and see if that Maxwell needed some help."

"Hang around. I'll see if I can hook you up with my boss." What had happened to his old friend? He'd been trail boss of big outfits and ramrod for others. Being out of work in Española was not like him.

"Who's he?" Collie Bill asked.

"Ain't a he, it's she." Slocum looked in approval at a fine-matched team of red mules that went past in a jig trot pulling a new red wagon loaded with supplies.

Collie Bill peered through slitted eyes at him. "You mean to tell me that you're working for a woman?"

Slocum rested his shoulder against the porch post and watched a young Hispanic woman cross the street. Fine-looking swing in her walk. He turned back to Collie Bill. "Yeah, she's been into it with some bunch called the Booster brothers. And some band of outlaws even killed her husband."

"Cal Booster in this deal somehow?"

"You know them?"

"Damn right, I know him and his brother Rip. Had a shoot-out with him and two of his rannies up in Dodge one time."

"Shame you didn't kill him then." Slocum pushed off the post and turned back to his friend. "I need to go check on her right now. Where's your pony?" Turning around in a half circle, he looked for a hitched horse. Collie Bill always rode a good one.

"Turned up lame. I was hoping you had some horseflesh I could borrow to get me over to Cimarron."

Slocum shook his head and dug out some silver cartwheels. "Go rent a pony. We'll go out and meet her and I'll introduce you."

Collie Bill hardly looked convinced. "I never put much stock in working for a woman."

"You're hungry, aren't you?"

"Yes."

"You're dead broke?"

"Yes. But I still ain't warm-blooded enough for the notion to start working for no woman."

Slocum gave him a shove. "Go rent the horse. I'll introduce you. It won't be bad."

"Damn you, Slocum, catch a man down and you want to use him." Collie Bill grinned.

"Any way I can. Go get a horse."

They started up the street on foot, Slocum leading Heck. Dodging rigs and freight wagons, he and Collie Bill headed for the sign marked LIVERY.

They reached the livery and Collie Bill went inside. Slocum wrapped his reins on the hitch rack and waited outside. The day had warmed up some, and he stood with his butt on the hitch rail, watching traffic go by.

A woman came running from around the building. "Help me! Help me!"

"What's wrong?"

"This man is beating my sister."

"Where?'

"At my casa."

"Is it her husband?"

"No."

They hurried around the building through the narrow space and crossed a street, the woman holding up her dress to hurry. "Only a little way. Oh, please save her."

On the move, Slocum felt for his gun out of habit. They crossed a yard of barking dogs, his sharp hiss making them back far enough away to let him and the woman pass. They rounded the corner of an adobe house, and from across the street he could hear a woman's wails coming from a small jacal.

He drew his gun and crossed the street, waving the woman back with the .44. The sounds of the victum's wailing and a man's cussing inside carried to Slocum as he passed a good sorrel horse standing hipshot under the small mesquite tree. He reached the open doorway with the six-gun in his fist, and spotted the man's broad back as he towered over the bloody-faced woman on the floor. It was Harvey Ryan.

He was ranting at her, and started kicking her. Slocum busted him over the crown of his hat with his pistol, and the big man's knees buckled. Looking horrified, the bloody-faced woman scurried away from him like a crayfish as he went down face-first.

Not taking a chance, Slocum jerked Ryan's gun out of its holster and stuck it in his own waistband. The other woman was already inside and on her knees, hugging the sobbing victim in her arms.

"*Gracias, señor. Gracias.* He would have killed her."

Slocum nodded and jerked the groggy Ryan by the collar to his knees. "You ain't getting the point of things. I warned you once. I'm short on patience."

Out of bleary eyes, Ryan looked up at Slocum. "This ain't none of your damn business."

"I'm making it mine. Now load your ass up on your horse and go back where you came from. You bother her again and I'll send you to hell for kicking your last woman."

"Who in the devil are you anyway?"

"The sumbitch that's going to kill you. Now get out of here."

Unsteady, Ryan got to his feet, holding his head. He reached for his six-gun and frowned. "Where's my gun?"

"You ain't getting it back. Get the hell out of here."

Ryan went peddling backward for the door. "You ain't heard the last of this—"

"If you don't make tracks, you will hear your last words on this earth. Now get out."

With some strain, Ryan mounted the sorrel and reined him up. "There will be another day for me and you."

"Buy a casket for yourself before you come. I ain't wasting a blanket on burying you." Slocum holstered his own .44 and turned back to the jacal.

The woman who had summoned him stood in the doorway.

He looked around to watch Ryan disappear on his horse and, satisfied, turned back to her.

"She's going to be all right. Thanks, Señor," the woman said. "I am sure he would have killed Maria here if you hadn't come."

"What goes on with 'em?"

"He was her lover. Then he began to tell her what she must do and not do." The woman shook her head and moved the coarse long hair back from her face with her fingers. "Finally, he said she should move into his casa. She knew then she would only be his slave, so she ran away, which made him mad."

"I see. I can't stay here. So tell Maria to be careful."

Collie Bill was coming up the street on a Roman-nosed bay, leading Heck and looking for Slocum. "What did you get into?" Bill asked.

"Some guy was beating up his girlfriend and I sent him packing. Long story."

With a tip of his hat for the lady, Collie Bill handed Slocum his reins. "Well, lucky for her you were around."

Slocum mounted and sat up in the saddle. "Maybe." Maybe he'd only prolonged Maria's problems. "Let's ride and go meet the boss." He booted Heck off in a hurry.

5

Slocum and Collie Bill found his boss coming down the road on the dancing gray a hundred feet or more ahead of the creaking *carreta*. Slocum glanced over, and noticed the flash of surprise on Collie Bill's face at the sight of Señora Peralta.

"The storekeeper is anxious for you to spend the night at his casa," Slocum said to her, sweeping off his hat.

She nodded and looked at his companion.

"This is Collie Bill Hankins. He's a good man. He'll ride along just in case."

She agreed to that and checked the stallion. "I will ride on to Española," she said. "We will leave at daybreak?"

"Fine. We can see the *carreta* safely into town. Oh, do you have an extra horse around here?"

"I am sure I can borrow one from Señor Goldfarb."

"Do that. We'll return it. Collie Bill's horse went lame."

"Of course. How unfriendly I must seem. Nice to meet you, Señor."

"Don't worry none about that, ma'am. I can see you have lots on your mind," Collie Bill said, and smiled.

"I do," she agreed, and galloped off on the hard-packed caliche road to Española.

In the early afternoon, they arrived at Goldfarb's walled compound along the ditch that watered the small fields and gardens during the valley's growing season. An older man named Felix showed them to the stables and the stout roan horse that his *patrón* was lending them. Collie Bill thanked the man, and said he needed to go get his things. He left on his new horse leading the rented one, to go back to town.

Slocum smiled. Obviously, his friend didn't want anyone changing their mind about the loan of the horse after riding the livery's dull bay for half of a day. It was a typical stable horse, mere transportation. The bull and oxen were put up and Diego went to take a siesta. Slocum found a spot to sit on a bench under a shower of golden cottonwood leaves. He was whittling idly on a stick when a young woman came past him in a swirl of skirts. In her arms she carried a small sack of sugar.

"You must be the pistolero she hired?" Her dark eyes inspected him as she paused before him and slightly swung her hips as if still walking.

He smiled at her. She was not a child. She was short and shapely enough. When he met her look, she glanced away toward the gate archway.

"Yes, sirree, and you must be the sugar lady," he said.

Her dark eyes turned back to him and took on a look of mischief. "You want some sugar?"

"You have some?"

She dried her palm on her dress, looking away from him. "I might have some."

"Where would you keep it?"

She lowered her voice. "Oh, go behind the stables to the small jacal. I will be there in a while. I must deliver this sugar, then I am off work."

"Good. We shall meet again."

She raised her gaze to the sky and tried to suppress her grin of excitement. "I hope so." Then she hurried off.

He whittled for a while, and then he tossed the piece of stringy cottonwood away. On his feet, he stretched his arms over his head as if tired and went for the stable. Parting the dusting and scratching reddish hens out in front, he went in the big open doors of the barn, which reeked of sweet alfalfa.

The floor was made of worn wood, and he went by the stabled teams and fine horses and to the back walk-through door. There he paused and studied the hayracks and iron dump rake parked outside. High in a pine tree, a Mexican mockingbird scolded him in a wren's tongue. Seeing nothing out of place, he headed for the shed the woman had spoken about. The door latch was on a string, with a peg tied on the end to keep it from being lost.

He lifted the latch and the door let sunlight fall on the floor. Cobwebs clung to the wall studs and were draped around the small four-pane window that cast its light on the cot. The narrow bed was covered with a large woven cotton blanket striped in black and white. He undid his gun belt and hung it on the lone chair so it would be handy.

He saw in his mind an image of her strolling toward the house, obviously not wishing to appear too anxious about their planned meeting. But hell, he could tell she was as anxious to get on with it as he was. He peeked out the small dirty window and saw no sign of her. Back beside the bed, he toed off his boots and sat on the mattress. He put his hat on the chair's corner post and lay back to relax.

He closed his eyes and fell asleep. The door latch's scratching sound and the woman's hard breathing woke him up. She closed the door and came across the room shedding her skirt.

"We don't have much time," she hissed at him, stepping out of the skirt and tossing it on the chair.

He smiled, looking at her shapely brown legs in the half-light as he undid his pants and belt. "What's wrong?"

"I must help with fixing supper. I only have a short time."

Out of his britches and standing with the cool air on his bare skin, he reached for her. His mouth parted her lips and her hands flew to his ears to cup his face so she could kiss him back.

She broke loose and pulled him after her to the bed. "My name is Carmaletia."

"Slocum."

"Yes, I heard your name." She was arranging herself underneath him, pulling up the blouse to expose her flat navel and the dark thatch of pubic hair. Spreading her legs apart, she squirmed and smiled at him, getting set for his penetration. "Maybe not too fast?"

"Oh, not so fast, huh?"

She raised her chin up and closed her eyes as he reached under to guide his stake inside her. "Oh, not too fast—"

His entry caused her to suck in her breath and clutch him. "Mother of God, you are big as a horse."

"You been fooling with a horse lately?"

"No, soft, small donkey ones." She sighed some more as he fought to plunge deep into her, and gathered up her legs for his entry.

"Yes. Yes," she cried, and with her legs doubled over on top of her, she rocked on her back as he poured his all to her.

Their world became a whirlpool sucking them deeper and deeper. Short on wind, drunk on passion's fire. His turgid dick stuffed her contracting walls until they both were dizzy, and then from behind the pained swollen head of his dick came a lava fountain that flew out and split him in two deep inside her.

She went faint and threw open her arms. He raised up enough and her legs unfolded, falling off on both sides of the bed. Hip to hip, they lay connected with his arms keeping some of his weight off her. He bent over and kissed her.

She raised her head up and looked around. "I must get back to work. She wants a fancy supper for your boss—"

He was busy slowly moving his half-full dick in and out of her. Her hand flew to her forehead as if she would swoon. "Again?"

"Again." He could feel the power returning to his tool as his hips began to get engaged with her. Yes, one more time for good measure.

6

That evening, he and Collie Bill went to a nearby cantina for supper. They were served a heaping platter of sizzling-hot chunks of fire-roasted beef, fried jalapeños and red peppers and onions, and a bowl of brown beans with a stack of fresh-made flour tortillas.

"I'm going to find a bath when we get through here," Slocum said. "I'm about tired of smelling myself."

"Hell, it ain't spring yet," Collie Bill said between bites off his rolled-up tortilla full of meat and trimmings.

"Winter or fall, after we eat I'm finding a barbershop and getting a shave and haircut." Slocum cut up some more of the chucks of meat on his plate.

"How is the food?" the waiter asked.

"Too good." Slocum laughed and nodded in approval. "I ate here very much, I'd be too spoiled to leave town."

"Yeah," Collie Bill agreed. "You tell that cook he is *muy grande*."

"I will tell him. You need more wine?"

"Sure, bring another bottle," Slocum said, nodding at a hesitant Collie Bill who, he figured, had not been eating that regular of late.

When the meal was completed, Collie started picking his teeth. "Now tell me about this sugar girl."

31

"I was minding my own business and she came by packing some sugar. I asked if she had some and she did."

Collie Bill snickered. "She wasn't bulldog ugly, potbellied, and a snaggle-toothed grandmother?"

"No, she ain't bad. Carmaletia. Works in the kitchen up there."

"Wonder when she gets through?"

"I don't know."

"Where does she live?"

"Damned if I know."

Collie Bill scowled at him. "You ain't much help."

"Hell, you never had no woman troubles that I can recall."

"I'm out of practice. I've had some setbacks."

Slocum raised his glass of wine. "Here's to better times."

"Yeah and Carmaletia." Collie Bill returned the toast.

Slocum found the barbershop that the waiter directed him to. An older man who introduced himself as Muygey smiled at him when he entered the small shop.

"What can I do for you, Señor?"

"Haircut, shave, and bath."

"Ah, I will tell my wife to heat the water. Have a seat."

When his hair was sheared and his face was scraped clean, Slocum rubbed the fresh alcohol-tinged skin and looked at himself in the mirror. Much better-looking than before. He followed Muygey into the back room and the steaming copper tub that awaited him.

"*Gracias,*" Slocum said, and the man excused himself to go out into the other room. Soon, Slocum was undressed and soaking in the hot water, his six-gun in the holster laid close by on the chair. The water felt good on his sore back.

A commotion in the barbershop made his senses quicken. He heard Muygey shout, "You can't go in there!"

Slocum filled his hand with the .44, shook it out of the holster, and cocked it as a man armed with a six-gun fought aside the curtain in the doorway. The explosion of Slocum's pistol and the attacker's shot, which went into the floor, made his ears ring.

Jumping out of the tub, water spilling all over, Slocum swept the curtain aside with his left hand and shoved the cocked gun ahead with his right. He rushed into the shop in time to see a fleeing man go out the front door. Muygey was on the floor, but looked only shaken. Outside in the growing darkness, the cold night air struck Slocum's bare skin as he realized he was stark naked save for the .44. No sign of the second gunman.

Inside, he wrapped a barber sheet around his waist. He joined the older woman kneeling on the floor, using a wet rag on Muygey's forehead.

"He all right?" Slocum asked her.

"It is only a scratch, Señor," she said.

"I could not stop them," Muygey said.

"You know that other guy?"

"I never saw them before."

"What's going on in here?"

Slocum looked up and saw the shotgun-packing marshal standing in the doorway with a frown on his face.

"The shooter is in there." Slocum indicated the curtain.

"Who is he?" The lawman stomped by in his heavy boots and pushed the curtain open.

Slocum helped Muygey up and nodded to his wife. "I'm finishing my bath."

"I am so sorry, Señor," the barber said.

"I'll be fine." Slocum kept the sheet wrapped around his waist, and drew some laughter from the onlookers filtering in as he went out back behind the curtain.

"He dead?" Slocum asked the marshal.

"If he ain't, he will be soon."

"You know him?" Slocum shed the sheet and climbed into the tub. "He sure upset my bathing."

The lawman looked at Slocum hard. "You kill a man and get right back in a bath?"

"Yes, and the water is getting cold. I paid a dime for it. Ten seconds later, I'd of been dead and he'd been miles away from here. I have no remorse for that bastard. He came to kill me."

"What's your name?"

"Slocum."

"Why do you figure he wanted you dead?"

"I have enemies in this world. I have no idea what they think. I have never seen him before. Who is he?"

"A drifter called Tom Parson. Been hanging around town. I figured he was looking for work and a quick buck."

"Anyone hang out with him?"

"I don't think so, but there's always others."

"You find out who hired him, I'll be back in a few weeks. I'll make it worth your time." Slocum stepped out and began to dry himself off. He ignored the men who had crowded in the room to look at the dead one, and began to put on his clothes.

"You a bounty man?" the marshal asked.

"No, but I don't like sloppy assassins."

"I'll do some checking. Boys, pack him down to the undertaker on the corner."

"He dead, Buster?" one man asked.

"He ain't, he soon will be the way he's leaking blood. Get in here. One get on each arm, one on each leg. Take him out of here."

Dressed, Slocum reloaded his .44 and strapped it on. He paid the protesting Muygey fifty cents and left the shop through the throng of curious faces. He walked the dark dirt street in the starlight, passing in and out of the deep shadows of the cotton-woods. Who wanted him dead? Ryan? Or was it some other old enemy who saw him passing through and wanted to even a score?

Maybe he'd know in a couple of weeks.

His bedroll was laid out on the hay in the barn and Collie Bill's was beside his—but no Collie Bill. With a smile, he sat down on his roll and pulled off his boots. Maybe Carmaletia had more time for his friend than she did for *him*. From the sounds of things, his old pal needed it worse than he did. What had he said? Some setbacks in his life?

Slocum soon fell asleep.

7

The next morning, they left for the village of Herman, crossing the freshly restored wooden bridge over the Rio Grande, and headed north. Herman was a small village on the irrigated land of the valley. Before they hit the road in the predawn light, Señora Peralta had spoken of a cousin who farmed up there and who would board them for the night.

After they crossed the newly replaced structure over the Rio Grande, Slocum and Collie Bill rode on to scout the road ahead.

"Who was that shooter last night?" Collie Bill asked when they were away from the others.

"The marshal said he was a drifter. His name was Tom Parson."

Collie Bill shrugged. "I don't know the name. Maybe if I'd seen his face, I'd'a known him."

"He was a hired gun. Kind of sloppy at it. May have been drunk."

"Damn," Collie Bill swore, looking back to check on the road. "A man can't take a bath without some ranny barging in, it is really getting tough."

"I'd rather know who hired him."

"Hell, man, you've got enemies from here to hell and back."

"I'd just like to know who they are. Well, how did you and Carmaletia get along last night?"

Collie Bill grinned. "Real nice lady. Real nice."

"Good. Let's ride. I want to look over this Herman before Señora Peralta gets there." They set their horses in a long lope down the empty road.

In a short while, they passed several freighters, their rigs parked beside the road, the men having breakfast and getting ready to leave. Many oxen teams stood around in yokes still to be hitched for their half-a-day pull. Several teamsters waved and shouted at Slocum and Collie Bill to be friendly.

Late morning, they found Herman with its church steeple, jacales, and cantina. They dismounted at the rack and wrapped their reins around the rail. At the last minute, Collie Bill said he was unsure about his borrowed horse staying tied, so he fashioned a halter on him and tied him instead with the rope.

"I sure want him to be here when we come out of that joint."

Slocum, with his back to the wall as he chewed on a match, agreed and pushed off, ready to go inside when his friend finished the job.

A woman with large breasts worked the bar. She swept the long black hair back from her face and smiled at them. "What can I do for you hombres?"

"Two beers," Slocum said, and leaned his elbow on the scarred bar.

"What do you do for excitement around here?" Collie Bill studied the painting of the fat nude woman on the back bar.

The woman working the bar laughed. "What does it look like?"

"Looks like she's going to get cold without her clothes." Collie Bill rubbed his sleeves.

She put their beers on the bar and glanced back at the nude. "No one has ever worried about her before." Then she laughed again.

"Hate to see anyone that pretty freeze."

"Go over by the fireplace," she said, still amused. "It is warmer over there."

"Much obliged," Slocum said, and headed for the hearth with his foamy mug. Finding a chair, he sat down before the small crackling fire, absorbing the heat of the small blaze and sipping on the brew.

Back at the bar, the woman bartender gave a loud laugh, and Slocum never turned around to see what she and Collie Bill were up to. Obviously, from the sounds, they were having a good time. He was more concerned about who'd hired that shooter Parson than anything else. Questions like that always bothered him, especially when there were hired guns after him.

His hat hanging on his shoulder by the string around his throat, Collie Bill came over and drew up a chair. He glanced back to be sure the woman wasn't close enough to hear him. "She ain't half bad."

"We'll be around here tonight."

"I know. I told her."

Slocum half-smiled. "Now that's settled."

Collie Bill leaned forward with his elbows on his knees, facing the radiant heat. "What about the Booster brothers?"

"What's her name?" Slocum asked.

"Silvia."

"Silvia, we need some information," Slocum said to the bartender, and waved her over.

"I am coming, *mis amigos.*"

She hurried over and drew up a chair between them. "What do you need to know?"

"Tell us about the Booster brothers."

Her face turned dark and her eyes became slits. *"Bastardos."* Then she spit in the fireplace ashes.

"Oh, I see you like them," Slocum said, and ducked.

"They come here and they hurt my girls. They shoot holes in my walls and get crazy drunk. They aren't fun, they are mean. You got to be pretty mean, no—to hurt some girl making love to you? Don't you?"

Slocum nodded. "How many are there?"

"Five when they came here."

"When were they here last?"

"A couple of months ago." She slapped her forehead and

pushed her hair back. "Oh, I got my shotgun out and told them never to come back in here no more."

"I guess they believed you?"

She nodded hard at him. "I would kill them if they ever come back here. I really would."

Collie Bill reached over and hugged her waist. "Which one was the worst? Cal or his brother?"

"They were all bad. That big one, that mulatto. They call him Sims, he is the one with the knife." She broke into a tirade of Spanish swear words.

When Slocum finished his beer, he excused himself and left Collie Bill to learn all he could about the Boosters. With a wink behind her back to his buddy, Slocum left the cantina. Outside, he stopped at a street vendor and bought some fresh-made meat-and-bean burritos from her. Then he rode Heck back south to find Señora Peralta. He was near halfway back to Española when he could hear the wagon's loud squeak, and he reined up in the road under the warming sun. Soon, she appeared, and he waited for her approach on the stallion.

"No problems?" he asked, handing her one of the newspaper-wrapped burritos.

She shook her head and smiled. "You will fatten me."

He shrugged. "I'll have much work to do that. I'll feed Diego and you can ride on to your cousin's."

"Where is he?" she asked, unwrapping her food. "The other man?"

"Finding out all he can about your enemies."

"Oh."

"You recall a mulatto in that raid?"

She stopped and blinked at him, her face paling some under her complexion. "Is that one in Herman?"

Slocum gave a shake of his head, and then he checked Heck. "I only heard of him today. His name is Sims."

She nodded. "What else did you learn?"

"Lots of people hate them."

"Lots of people fear them, too."

"Eat your food." He indicated the burrito. "You will need your strength."

"I will owe you lots of money for your food service." She held up her burrito.

"About forty cents so far," he said.

"How much interest do you charge?"

"That's the catch. We can talk this evening about what we've learned. I'll see Diego and the King on into town and we can meet you at your cousin's. We'll be there in a few hours."

"Very good. We should be back at the ranch in two more days."

"No rush. Be careful. You do have a gun?"

"*Sí*. I can use it."

"Good. Remember, use it first if you're threatened. To wait is too late."

"Cruel men know that, don't they? They know it well?"

"That you won't shoot?"

She nodded. "Yes, they know that, don't they? 'She is a woman, she won't shoot me.' "

"Don't ever threaten. Shoot them. They'll respect that."

Between small bites, she nodded as if deep in thought. "It is not easy to shoot a man."

"Never is. But you have to figure, it is him hurting me or me shooting him."

"For a man, that must be much easier. Isn't it?" For the first time, she looked straight at him, her brown eyes large pools of liquid.

"Not really. But there is no time to think."

The trip into Herman was uneventful. Slocum found Collie Bill chewing on a straw and seated on a nail keg waiting for them when they drove up to the house, outbuildings, and corrals under towering golden cottonwoods at the end of the lane. Several black dogs barked at their arrival, and a man came to greet them.

"I am Raule Tomas. Welcome to my place, Señor."

"Slocum's mine. Glad to meet you." He dismounted and shook the man's calloused hand.

"You may put your horse in the corral, there is hay for him. I will go and show Diego where to put the *toro* and his oxen."

"Thank you," Slocum said, and began to pull loose the latigos to his cinches.

"Well, I learned one thing." Collie Bill was looking around to be sure they were alone when he joined Slocum.

"What is that?"

"Boosters are charging people with cattle for their protection. Probably her, too. But they still steal from everyone. There is some mining going on up in Colorado and they are herding the stolen cows up there. The market is good and with no expenses but the drive, they're making lots of money."

"What about brand inspectors? Colorado surely has them." Slocum lifted the saddle and blankets off Heck's back. He tossed the saddle over the corral top rail and then strung the pads out to dry.

"They're venting the brands like they'd bought them and putting a road brand on them."

"That's one way. But still, isn't anyone complaining?"

"No, they've burned out or killed anyone who reported them. Didn't take much of that to shut folks up."

"I suppose the complainers are buried, huh?"

"They disappear." Collie Bill nodded. "What're your plans?"

"I'm not certain. Get the bull delivered and then we can look at the señora's situation." He led Heck through the gate and slipped off the bridle. Did her husband object to the Boosters' tactics?

"I mean, we may be getting ourselves into a hornet's nest," said Collie Bill.

"I understand, but she didn't hire me to solve all her problems—for now, only to get the bull to her place safe."

"I think this may be a larger deal than we thought."

"You wanting out?"

"Ha. Me riding a borrowed horse and broker than a peon? Ain't no way I want out."

"Good, we'll figure this out sooner or later. Now that we know they're rustling to supplement their living on the high side."

Collie Bill nodded. "Maybe one of us ought to ride up to Colorado and look that over?"

"Wouldn't be a bad idea after we get the señora home."

"Couple of days?"

Slocum agreed. "We should be at her casa. But if they're shutting up the folks that report them, they've got spies around here. There ain't no telegraph wire strung around here."

"Wonder who that would be." Collie Bill took off his hat and scratched his head. "So we've got to watch out for them and their spies."

"Exactly." Slocum saw Tomas at the house, waving at them. That must mean food was ready. It wouldn't be easy finding the spies working for the Boosters. But someone knew who they were and those someones were out there. He needed to use them to his advantage. But how?

8

The morning came fast. Slocum's eyes were dry with grit as he rode in the frosty cold, wrapped in a blanket. It damn sure wouldn't be this cold in San Antonio. Besides, if he'd been there, he'd probably have shared his warm bed the night before with some sweet-smelling lover. He looked off at the sawtooth peaks in the east, purple with the approaching dawn. *Damn.*

"We can stay at the Flores Ranch tonight," Perla said, riding her gray between him and Collie Bill. "Then we will be at my place the next day."

"Good, King Arthur must be tired of the long ride." Slocum shared a grin past her at Collie Bill before he looked back at her with a serious expression on his face. "How many cattle are they stealing from you?"

She hunched her shoulders under her heavy coat. "I don't know. I only have some boys left as ranch hands."

"It's a shame to raise cattle for rustlers."

"They need me this way. They need the ranchers to provide them with cattle. They steal some, but they don't raid your ranch."

"Your husband fought them?"

She swallowed and nodded. "I told him he was foolish. A hundred times. I wish he had listened."

"So now they help themselves to your cattle and no one complains."

"Something like that. You don't understand."

"Why did you hire us?"

She checked her prancing gray. "They are not the only bad ones on this road."

Slocum shared a nod with Collie Bill, who showed by his grim face that he understood her concern. "It's a bad road," Slocum said.

"Yes, there is no one for miles, and outlaws rob the stages and the poor people who travel it all the time."

"We'll stick close today. We'd like to—Collie Bill and I'd like to stop this rustling."

She gave him a sharp look. "And end up dead?"

"Señora, we like living too well to have that happen." Collie Bill laughed and smiled at her.

"So did my husband."

"Ma'am," Slocum said. "We'd like to work for you and settle this business."

"They would come down on the ranch again." He dark eyes darted in search of an answer from either of them. "I can't risk that happening. Not again."

"I can't say they won't. But they need to be stopped."

"At what price? Hurting my people again?"

"I can't tell you that," Slocum said.

Warily, she shook her head. "I will pay you to get my bull home safely. I can't risk going against them."

"That's your final word?"

She nodded and drew back into her shell. Slocum felt he and Collie Bill could have been riding by themselves. No doubt she was dead set against them doing anything to help her. He wasn't halfway convinced, though, that he could simply ride out of there leaving Peralta's widow at the mercy of those outlaws.

At noontime, they stopped by a small spring-fed creek to eat some tamales she had brought from her cousin's. The golden canopy of the cottonwood leaves and being down in the canyon out of the wind gave them some warmth. Slocum and Collie Bill were squatting at a distance from her eating their food.

"You figure she'd blow up like that?" Collie asked under his breath.

"I wasn't sure how she'd react when the time came. She'd never committed herself aloud to that plan. All she'd asked for was us to get that bull home. The rest I made up in my mind, I guess." Slocum shook his head and took another bite of his tamale.

"I reckon they taught her a hard lesson the night they killed her husband and tore up the ranch."

"And raped her, too."

"I can see her not wanting that again."

"But they done it once. What's to keep them from doing it again?" Slocum asked.

"I'll be damned if I know."

"Hold tight, we've got some riders coming," said Slocum. He rose and studied the three men approaching on tough-looking mustangs.

Collie Bill rose, too.

The men were dressed in the garb of ranch hands, unshaven, looking hard first at Señora Peralta, then at Slocum and Collie Bill. It was their contemptuous faces that put Slocum on edge. These three—from the youngest, a boy with fuzzy blond whiskers, to the older ones, including the leader with the eye patch and his white and black stubble—were all bullies, all backed by the guns that they wore on their hips.

"What's your name?" One-Eye asked the señora.

She began, "My name is—"

"You don't have to tell these rannies anything," Slocum said, interrupting and stepping into the center of the ring. He waved her back. "You boys are a little short on manners, ain't ya?"

"Huh, who the hell are you?" One-Eye asked as he dismounted.

"Not that it is important, but my name is Slocum. Now, you boys pack up and get out of here."

The leader started for his gun, then reconsidered. The kid and the other man were already backing away.

"It ain't a good day to die, mister," Slocum said. "'Cause we ain't burying you. We'll let the buzzards do that." Slocum advanced on the man, and he began to retreat, too.

"You can only push a man so far—"

"What do they call you?"

"Davis."

"Well, Davis, get on your horse and get the hell out of here. Next time, take your hat off when you speak to a lady."

One-Eye took the reins from the kid, who was still mounted with a look of longing to be out of there written on his face. Red-faced and angry, One-Eye pointed his finger at Slocum. "I ever catch you or your gunfighting buddy there alone, I'll blow your asses off."

"What about today, Davis? Try it."

Davis shook his head slightly, never taking his single eye off Slocum's gun hand until he was mounted. "You ain't seen the last of me."

"Better forget it," Slocum said, and watched them ride off.

"Señora?" Collie Bill called out to her as the three galloped away. "Were they members of the gang that raided the ranch?"

She looked pale under the flat-crown hat as she shook her head. "I don't think so. All of those men wore flour-sack masks—" She shook her head in defeat.

Satisfied those three were gone, Slocum went over and took her by the arm. He motioned for her to sit on a dead log lying on the ground. "I'm sorry to upset you, but those men were bullies, and any show of weakness and they'd've done what they wanted."

She nodded that she understood as she chewed on her lower lip. "I hope I am not the cause of your death or his."

"That's not your worry. We're big boys and we can figure out the rest." He turned to Collie Bill. "You seen them before?"

"No, but five'll get you ten they've been in on the stage robberies up here."

"Been many of them?" Slocum asked.

"Most every time the coach comes down. Parties unknown shot a Wells Fargo man in the back a week ago."

"It's a shame, this is nice country," Slocum said, looking at the pine-and-juniper land around them. Good grass and several live water creeks coming out of the mountains in the west and rushing toward the Rio Grande should have made it fine ranching country. Still might be that if the Booster brothers and a few more sorry outfits like them were run out of that part of New Mexico.

"You feeling ready to ride?" he asked her.

"Yes." Her composure returned, and she took the reins from Collie Bill and thanked him. She set out with a wave to Diego, and they all mounted up.

"You almost broke through her shield," Collie Bill said in the saddle, reining his roan up. Then, with a big grin, he booted his horse out.

Slocum shook his head and swung back to check on Diego. "Everything all right?"

"*Sí, señor*. Hee-yah, get up," he said to his team, and the axle began to creak.

For a long moment, Slocum sat Heck and looked back down the road to make sure those three were gone and didn't try to sneak back for a potshot. Cowards like that were famous for doing such things. Another day and a half and they should be at the señora's ranch according to her. Then she could decide what she wanted done about the Boosters.

Satisfied that the three riders were gone for the moment, Slocum reined Heck around and rode to catch up with Collie Bill and escape the ear-piercing creak of the axle.

"Where were you headed next?" Collie Bill asked when Slocum joined him.

"I was planning to use the Spanish Trail and go west."

"If I could, I'd've been in San Antonio, warming my butt in the sun."

Slocum nodded. He had the same idea as he was swept by the cold breeze that even the full sun couldn't warm. "Why can't you?"

Collie Bill smiled. "I was down in Euvalde and found me a sweet—" He lowered his voice. "Señorita by the name of Rita. Aw, hell, Slocum, she was, you know, you know what I mean, a shapely little coffee-skin border girl. Well, her and me'd been on a three-day party. We were polka-ing at this fandango and a big man wearing a star butted in and told me that she was his girl. And asked where in the hell we'd been.

"I told him to stick the moon in his ass so he could spit out stars. He grabbed for his gun, and that was a bad mistake for both of us. I shot him and he fell down like a poled steer. Women were screaming bloody murder. I jumped out an open window. Time to scratch gravel. I'd shot a lawman, right or wrong. Found the first horse I came to and rode away."

"They have a poster out for you?"

"I never looked to see it."

Slocum nodded. "Bet you could go back to San Antonio and they'd never know you."

"There's a widow gal up in the hill country. She's from Norway. I ever figure out how, I'd slip back down there and see if she was still single."

"Maybe that's what you need to do."

Collie Bill used his finger to scratch under his shirt collar. "But I sure don't want a necktie party instead of a wedding."

They both laughed.

Later in the afternoon, they rode with Señora Peralta.

"We can stay tonight at the Flores Ranch. Manuel was a friend of my husband," she said.

"He have a big ranch?" Collie Bill asked.

"No, he has a stage station and some irrigated land to grow hay and corn on. His wife Juanita is my good amigo. They work very hard, and I only get to see her once in a while."

Slocum nodded. They'd passed two parked freight outfits that were headed north and had already stopped for the day to graze their stock. Feeding the *carreta* oxen grain at night spared Slocum and his party from having to stop that much. But after six to seven hours on the move each day, the freighters had to stop to let their oxen graze the rest of the day. This meant that most of the forage near the road was eaten down and the oxen had to be driven off to find feed. This was why the trains had a scout to ride ahead and look for the grass and water to make the next day's stop.

Slocum was grateful he wasn't scouting for one of those outfits. In no time at all their snail's pace would bore him to death.

Riding along with Señora Peralta was nice enough for him.
Was anyone else going to harass them? One Hereford bull
hardly seemed worth the fuss. Slocum shook away the notion
and looked over the tall mountains that hemmed them in. Be
nice up there if it was summertime.

9

Flores Ranch and Stage Station was in an open valley surrounded by pines on the hills. When Slocum and the others
topped the last rise, he could see the layout along the creek.
The brown corn stubble and green alfalfa fields were fenced
off by post and rail and bordered by bunchgrass and purple
sagebrush. Obviously, Flores was a neat farmer.

The land around his farmed acreage proved boggy, with
some small creeks and marsh grass webbing the valley. In
places, the main road was paved with pine logs to cross the
softer spots.

A gray-haired Hispanic man came out of the building and
hugged Señora Peralta.

Then the clean-shaven man in working clothes shook hands
with Slocum and Collie Bill. "Come inside and eat. The stage
is due in a half hour and they will eat our leftovers."

Slocum guessed him to be in his forties. He was an open
sort of a fellow who looked and acted genuinely concerned
about the señora. Flores's wife Juanita was half his age, a
short brown-skinned woman who smiled at her guests' arrival
and then hurried off for the food. She had a figure that would
catch any man's eye.

Two small children played on the floor in the dining room.
Slocum excused himself and Collie Bill. They went outside

and used the stinking outhouse in back. As they stood shoulder to shoulder draining their bladders in the holes under the low roof, Collie Bill said, "Nice outfit. He's got some stage income and a good farm. I ought to have found me a deal like this."

"You ain't too old to start," Slocum said, buttoning his pants.

"Hell, I've tried it a few times. Twice in Texas—and I met a gal had this homestead in Kansas. Whew, she was a big ole gal, but she had a body made like any man wanted. Her old man had got kicked in the head by a mule and died." Collie Bill shook his head in wonderment. "Old buddy, she could've screwed a pump handle to death."

"What happened?"

"I woke up one morning before daylight, got up, and had me this urge to run. Her corn was laid by and there was new ground to break for the coming year. I just saddled my old hoss and left. Got drunk in Baxter Springs just trying to forget that fine body I'd run off and left. Hell, I must of got into too many fights, ended in jail, lost my horse, saddle, and gear, and thirty days later, I hitched a ride back to Texas in a chuck wagon with that Bernelly outfit." Collie Bill dropped his head. "Dumb, dumb, dumb. That was the sorriest thing I ever did, and every time since then when I get me a hard-on alone in bed, I'm reminded of her."

"There's women like that in this world." Slocum washed his hands in the basin set out for them on the back porch. The wind had a nip. He needed a heavier coat.

"Either the stage is early or there's people coming." Collie Bull stuck his head around the corner. When he turned back, he hitched the gun on his hip and gave Slocum a serious look. "I think the Booster gang has arrived."

Slocum hung the stiff towel on a nail. "How many?"

"Four."

"What makes you think it's them?"

"Red bandannas for hatbands. Silvia mentioned it. They all wear 'em. I guess so they don't shoot each other."

Slocum nodded, drew his Colt, and checked the five rounds in the chambers, then shut the gate and reholstered it. It might be a good day for such things. "I guess it's a good day to meet them."

"Yeah. My paw always said don't put off today what you need to do."

Slocum grinned. "Good advice. Looks like today is the day."

From the corner of the clapboard stage stop, he could see the riders coming in a trot out of the south. He and Collie Bill went inside. They both took coffee and stood at the back of the room. Perla was off in the kitchen with Flores's wife Juanita.

When Perla appeared in the doorway, Slocum cleared his throat to get her attention. Then when she looked at him, he shook his head at her. She nodded and turned to go back in the side shed that housed the cooking facility. Collie Bill shared a nod of approval with him.

Juanita called the two small children into the kitchen with her and Perla.

Outside, the riders were talking among themselves with lots of bravado. Slocum could hear words and the cling of spurs and the drum of boot heels on the porch. A tall black man filled the doorway, ducking his head to enter.

"Well . . ." He paused and considered the two of them. "Howdy there. Guess you's two be new in dis country?"

"New enough," Slocum said.

"Well, brother, we just passing through. Don't want no trouble and we be looking for some food is all we's want. Right, boys?" he said over his shoulder.

"Yeah," came the chorus.

"I can feed them," Juanita said, coming from the kitchen. "Come in. Have a seat. I have some pork roast and some potatoes."

The man removed his hat and put it on a peg. "You's heard her, boys. Get in here." He shifted the gaze of his bloodshot brown eyes back to Slocum and Collie Bill. "My name's Sims."

"Slocum's mine and that's Collie Bill."

"Pleased to meetcha." He eased his huge frame down on the bench. He was still taller sitting than the three hands standing: a pimple-faced kid, an older man with a white mustache, and a bald-headed man. "That's Kid, that's Kemp, and that's Baldie. He ain't hard to tell." Sims laughed. Not a funny laugh, but a cold one.

Slocum rested his butt against the wall and blew on his coffee. Collie Bill stood ten feet to his left doing the same. How long they'd stand them off, Slocum had no way to measure—time would tell.

Juanita quickly brought the heaping dishes and served the outlaws. Then she poured them coffee in mugs.

With a biscuit in his left hand and ready to fork in the food with his other, Sims cut Slocum a hard look. "Better eat with us."

"We've ate," Slocum lied.

"Sure be good food, huh?" Sims elbowed the younger one.

"Yeah," he said with his mouth full.

With his fork, Sims pointed at the door. "That be you's new bull out there."

"We're looking after it."

"I guess that lady owns him be proud to see him."

"I guess she will."

"Hey! This sure is good grub, Mrs. Flores."

She came out of the kitchen, acknowledged his compliment, and refilled their cups.

The others made small comments to each other, barely audible to Slocum, who held his cup out for a refill, too. She nodded grimly to him and then went over to fill Collie Bill's.

"You figuring on planting you-self around here?" Sims asked, ready to swill down some coffee.

"Depends."

"And what that be?"

"Who my neighbors are."

"Oh, you might not like them."

"Might not."

"Be a pure shame to live by someone you didn't like."

"It would be."

'Well, we's got work to do. Finish up here, boys, we got's some miles to make. Better shake our hocks." He went for his hat and the boys began to get up.

Sims let the others file outside, then put on his hat, sucking on his teeth. "Guess we'll meet again."

"Maybe you should pay her for the meal," Slocum said.

A slow smile parted Sims's thick dark lips. "My, my, I 'most forgot." He tossed two coins on the table with a wave.

Perla appeared in the side doorway after Sims went outside. Slocum waved her back into the kitchen. It wasn't over yet. He and Collie Bill went to the front door, and then out on the porch to watch the big man mount a horse that stood seventeen hands high.

"See's you's boys," Sims said with a wave, and rode off with the others.

Collie Bill's blue eyes flashed when he whirled to face Slocum. "You thinking like I was?"

Slocum nodded. "Yeah, I figured that cocky Kid might try to take some shots at King Arthur, too."

The white-faced bull bellowed loudly, and then Slocum and Collie Bull turned to go inside. At least the bull was still alive to bawl. Slocum took off his hat and slapped his leg with it. He looked up and met Perla's concerned gaze.

"I am sorry you had to take such a chance for me," she said.

"Wasn't no chance for us. If they'd blowed up at Collie and me, there'd been a bunch of boot toes pointing at the sky."

"Those men are killers." A frown creased her smooth forehead. "You don't know them."

"Back shooters and women abusers. Aside from Sims, there ain't a one in that outfit could hit a barn door. Right, Collie?"

"The way I figure it, they were counting on him, too."

"How many more of them are there?" Slocum asked her.

"The two brothers, a sister is all I know. Unless they've hired more."

"Those the men raided your ranch?"

She shook her head. "The gang raided the ranch all had masks. We didn't know them. I think that bunch fled. They probably were worried about the law getting after them."

"Probably so." Slocum turned back to Collie Bill, who was standing in the doorway. Why did people always say the raiders were masked, he wondered.

Collie Bill nodded. "Sims is the main one they got. Damn big. He's six feet eight if he's an inch."

Flores was out of breath when he arrived at the headquarters. "I had to check on some ditch water. I was on my way in the back. Did they harm anyone?"

Slocum shook his head, and wondered why at this time of year a man had to worry about ditch water. But it wasn't his concern. "They ate and ran."

"Good," Flores sighed.

"Wonder where they were headed." Collie Bill held a toothpick in his hand.

"Your food is ready," Juanita announced, holding two heaping plates. "*Gracias* to both of you."

"Juanita," Collie Bill said to her. "You ever need you another man, just call on me." He sat down on the bench with his back to the wall and looked in amazement at all the food. "I'd work for my keep here."

They all laughed.

Perla refilled their coffee cups. Slocum had taken his first bite when the stage driver's bugle in the distance told him the coach was coming. Flores rushed off to get the horses ready for the change, and the quiet Diego went to help him. Slocum savored his food, and Perla rook a seat opposite him. She fidgeted with putting sugar in her coffee. She acted undecided about being there. When she did settle down, she chewed on her lower lip and glanced several times at the door.

"That taste good?" Slocum asked in a low voice.

"What?" She blinked at him.

"You're going to chew a hole in that lip of yours."

She ran her hands over her legs under the table. "I'm sorry."

"No, you're upset. Those men are gone. They won't ever hurt you again."

"How do you know that?"

"I'm going to see to it."

"I don't want that."

"Let me handle it my way."

She shook her head. "Losing my husband was bad enough."

He dropped his gaze to his heaping plate and went to eating

his food. There was no convincing her. He'd let things settle, then he'd start culling Booster's men out. The first ones would be easy. Then he'd handle the rest of them. The food did taste good.

The stage passengers came in the room. Perla fled to the kitchen. The three men in suits stomped in looking road-weary and hard-eyed from the long ride. He didn't know the three drummers, but the thin dark-headed woman wrapped tight in the long black cape, he recognized. Mary Murphy, a gambler he knew from Kansas cow towns. She always acted like she could wrap up in her clothes and disappear. When she took a seat on the opposite side of the table, she never showed any sign that she'd recognized him.

Where was she headed? Then a strong musky smell struck his nose. An aroma that wasn't particularly inviting to him. Then he realized that Murphy was experiencing *the curse of Eve*. It must be her. The poor woman was riding in a stage full of men with few or no conveniences for herself along the way.

She ate nothing and then excused herself. He watched her hit the back door and go outside. He took his coffee cup to the front door. When he heard the outhouse door slam open, he stepped out and around to the side of the building to speak to her.

She pulled the cape tight around herself and looked at him with sharp eyes. "What in hell's name are you doing up here?"

"Working. Where're you headed?"

She gave him a peeved look, drew the cape tighter around herself, and raised her chin. "I didn't like Colorado and some of the people up there."

He'd forgotten what a bitch she could be, especially during her time. "You get crossways with the boss?"

"You could say that. I fuck who I want and when I want them. I ain't some damn orphan that he could poke any time his dick flowered. Besides, there isn't much gold crossing the felt up there."

"Do I know him?"

"The name he used up there was Anderson." She folded her arms and quickly swept back a wisp of hair from her face. "Vince Anderson."

"Well, Murph, where next?"

"Tombstone. They say it's wide-open."

"Have a nice stage ride."

She looked around and then made a face. "Shame there ain't a place here, we could get it on. I always liked you when I felt the lousiest. Might make this damn stage ride easier to take."

He shook his head. "No place here. Good luck to you in Tombstone."

"Come down there. We'll renew our acquaintances. I could always stand a good long night with you."

"They're rustling cattle around here. Taking them up to Colorado and selling them to a butcher."

"To a German named Raunald Krone who has the slaughterhouse. I dealt some cards with him. He don't know shit about cards, but he makes lots of money in the butcher business up there."

"The stage is about ready to haul out."

She looked around. "Guess you're busy working?"

He nodded. "Why?"

"Well, I could take the next stage if you had a bed to fuck me in."

"I've got a blanket."

"Screw that. Too cold for that crap. Besides, you'd ruin my back on some rocks under it. Don't take any bad pussy."

He nodded. His nose full of her thick musky smell, he watched her close herself in the cape and hurry away to get on the stage. With a chuckle in his throat, he went back to the porch—whew, he was glad she'd gotten aboard the coach.

The Booster brothers and Sims were still out there. A force to be reckoned with sooner or later if he stayed in this country. He, Collie Bill, and Diego would deliver the bull the next day to Perla's ranch. Then he could decide on what to do.

Murphy's sour smell was still in his nose.

10

A thick frost coated everything before sunup. Slocum had a fire going when Collie Bill crawled out from under his blankets and came to the heat. Both squatted down holding out their hands to warm them in the radiant heat, using blankets slung over their backs for coats.

"Son of a bitch, it's cold. I'd give my eyeteeth for some long handles," Collie Bill swore when he backed up to sit on a log. "I'd swear we're stupid being up here and winter coming on. Why, the snow'll be butt-deep on a tall mule one of these mornings."

"What do you think?"

"Think? I can't think. I'm up here on a borrowed horse, living off my friend and penniless."

"You've been in rougher deals."

"I damn sure have, but I swore that it would never happen to me again."

"She's coming," Slocum said under his breath, and both of them rose to meet Perla.

"Good morning," she said. "I think Diego and I can make it up to the ranch today from here. I thought I should pay what I owe you."

His hat in his hand, Slocum nodded. "We'd like to see you

make it home since we came this far." He turned back in the fire's light to Collie, and Collie nodded agreement.

"That won't be necessary," she said. "We can make it fine from here."

"There's the matter of the roan horse." Slocum turned to Collie Bill, who nodded again.

"I can pay my cousin for him on my next trip south and make you a bill of sale for him. My cousin won't mind. Is the roan horse and ten dollars enough?" she asked Collie Bill.

"Oh, yes, ma'am. I'm plumb grateful. I haven't done that much work for you."

"Here is the ten."

"Thanks."

She turned back to Slocum. "I owe you fifty, right?"

"Yes, ma'am, but—" Slocum wanted to protest.

"No, we agreed to that amount. I live by my word."

"It's too much is what I mean."

"I agreed to pay you fifty dollars." She handed him the money. "My thanks to both of you."

Slocum stood with the money in his hand and shook his head at her. Ignoring his concern, she turned and headed for the stage building in the shadowy light.

Collie Bill grinned. "Broke one minute, and the next I've got a good horse and ten bucks in my pants pocket. You can't beat that."

Slocum tossed another pine knot on the fire. "I'd've felt lots better if she'd took my offer to let us get rid of those Boosters."

"I savvy that. What are you going to do now?"

"Find a pair of long handles, a wool-lined coat, some gloves, and then I'll see what I need to do."

"Where you going to find all that?"

"Right up the road in Colorado. There's stores up there."

Collie Bill gave him a disappointed look. "You're aiming to winter here, ain'tcha?"

"I aim to find out all I can about the Boosters and their business."

"They ain't worth freezing your ass off up here for that." Collie Bill clapped his hands on his legs. "But if you're going to do that, guess I'll hang on awhile. Why do you reckon she paid us off here? Ashamed for us to see her place, or has she got other problems?"

"She's a loner. I don't know what she was like before they killed her husband, but she's sure private now."

"Yeah," Collie Bill agreed. "She's damn sure a keep-to-herself woman. Ain't no flirt in her." He shook his head and hunkered under his blanket.

Diego came up about then under a blanket. "Cold today."

"We've already done found that out," Collie Bill said, and laughed. "Guess we part ways here this morning."

"Where do you go?"

"We ain't sure. She paid us off and thanked us. Said you two'd make it fine the last leg of the journey."

Diego stood close to the fire and warmed his fingers. "I am sorry to hear that. I had hoped she would hire you and more men. Maybe you could have run the Boosters and their bunch out of here."

"She don't want that," Slocum said.

"She is afraid. Her husband was forming a posse to do that when that masked gang came and killed him and raided the ranch."

Slocum nodded. "That may be why."

"It sure makes sense. Them coming in here yesterday like they owned the place probably reminded her of all that, too," Collie Bill said.

Diego agreed. "What will you do?"

"Go look for gold, I guess." Slocum added more wood to the fire. "She don't want us to help her."

"Ah, it will soon be too cold to do much anyway."

The man was probably right. Once Slocum was dressed in some winter clothing, he could go look over the Booster deal. He planned to do that, unsure what Collie Bill might want to do.

"When're we leaving for Colorado?" Collie Bill asked.

"After we talk Juanita out of breakfast."

"Good, I thought you might starve me." Collie Bill fell in with him and they went inside.

"Good morning." Juanita flashed her white teeth at them

from the stove where she cooked in the side room. "How long have you two been up?"

"Since it got too cold to sleep," Collie Bill said, sliding the blankets off his shoulders.

She looked them over as if sizing them up. "I have some coats might fit you, but . . ."

"What is it?" Collie Bill asked.

"They belonged to dead men. I save them. When a passenger is shot in a robbery, the driver brings them to me and I mend them."

"Wouldn't bother me." He looked at Slocum.

"Heavens, I ain't particular." Slocum shook his head.

"They have bullet holes in them."

"Ain't no ghosts in them?" Collie Bill asked with a grin.

Ignoring his question, she handed him a plate with a stack of flapjacks. "Here, you two can start on these. I'll go up and get the coats. They're in a trunk in the house."

Skirt in hand, she started for the side door and stopped. "Go eat those. I can make more."

They smiled and did as they were told. Her fresh butter and huckleberry jam made the pancakes mouth-watering, especially washed down with the rich hot coffee.

Collie Bill looked around. "Guess her man doesn't get up early."

"Guess not."

"A man got a woman works as hard as she does sure is lucky."

Between forking in food, Slocum looked over at Collie Bill. "Didn't you ride off and leave one like her?"

"Most foolish damn thing I ever did."

"Maybe someday you'll get another chance."

"Naw." Collie Bill shook his head. "A man only gets a chance like that once in a lifetime."

They both looked up at the sound of the side door opening. "I got them."

They both rose as Juanita burst in with two coats. One was a red and white plaid woolen coat, the other a sheep-lined leather one.

"Which one you want?" Collie Bill asked Slocum.

"The leather one if I'm getting a choice and it'll fit." Slocum took it from her, and Collie Bill was already putting on the plaid coat.

"This fits great," Collie Bill said, smoothing out the sleeves. "Warm, too. How's yours?"

"Made for me." Slocum buttoned up the deer-horn buttons and hunched his shoulders under the thick coat. He felt warm for the first time in days. Then he swung it off and hung it on a wall peg.

"What do we owe you?" he asked, turning back to her.

She shook her head. "When you made those bullies pay for their lunch yesterday, I owed you those coats. It never was the money. It was the fact they acted like I owed them their meals."

At the sound of the back door opening, she put her finger to her mouth and shook her head to dismiss any more conversation. Slocum and Collie Bill went back to eating their pancakes. Diego came into the dining area and joined them. She delivered more pancakes and a plate of thin-sliced fried pork.

"Where do you two go next?" she asked.

"Colorado for a look-see," Slocum said between bites.

"You two better eat lots. It's a long ride to Colorado," she said, amused.

"Ah, someone will feel sorry for us along the way," Slocum teased.

She laughed and headed for the cook shed. "I bet they will. You two could eat on your looks about anywhere."

"Good news to me," Collie Bill said. Even Diego laughed.

They thanked her again, left, and saddled their horses. Diego had already saddled the gray stallion for Perla. Tied to the corral, it acted impatient to get home, pawing the dirt.

Perla soon came from the low-roofed house, slapping her chaps with a quirt. Slocum watched her stride toward them in the yellow first light. Lots of woman under that leather clothing—he appreciated his own new garb. Juanita had washed most of the bloodstains out of the wool lining and stitched the hole in the back shut.

"So you are off?" Perla asked.

"Yeah, we were fired this morning," Slocum said.

Her eyes quickly narrowed. "I only hired you to—"

"Tell me one thing, Señora. Did me standing up to Sims yesterday speed up our firing?"

Her face grew very blank. "Think what you want. Diego, bring the bull home."

She unhitched the gray, vaulted in the stirrup, and swung her leather-clad leg over the saddle. With her boots in the stirrups, she jabbed him sharply with her spurs and left them.

"I'd say you plumb pissed her off, ole buddy."

Slocum agreed and grinned at his pal. "I sure did, didn't I?"

"You did a real good job at that."

Why was she so opposed to him doing something about those "regulators"? Someone needed to stop them. If it wasn't him, it would be someone else. Maybe he'd never understand Perla of the Rio Grande. No telling. She was one woman he'd not loosened up one bit. There weren't many he couldn't get close to, but Perla Peralta was sure one of them.

They swung by the kitchen, thanked Juanita again, and then rode north.

11

Pagosa Springs' businesses crowded the stinking, steaming springs. A smell of rotten eggs and fog from the hot thermals swept the street and filled Slocum's nostrils. He and Collie Bill stopped at Grayson's livery and boarded their horses. It was cloudy, and Slocum expected snow anytime. He reserved two bunks for them in the livery's bunkroom—then they set out to find some food.

Despite Juanita's promise, they'd found their three-day ride uneventful and without much food service along the way. They headed across the street for the café. Slocum turned up his collar as he dodged through the buggy and horse traffic. The sun was dying behind the thick cloud bank.

"I could eat a horse," Collie said, leading the way inside.

"Or a full-grown grizzly?" Slocum grinned. Their meals had been slight on the road. Moving along without any chance to hunt, they'd eaten lots of tough pepper jerky out of his saddlebags. The notion of real food appealed to Slocum and his pard as well. It was all they'd talked about coming into town in the late afternoon.

"Seen a menu?" a plain-looking waitress asked.

"What's on it, darling?" Collie Bill asked, looking up at her.

"Elk, beef, or ham." She cocked her hip to the side with her right hand poised on it. In her thirties, she had a hard red face and a long nose. The rest of her body sagged.

"Good elk?"

"They shot it yesterday above town."

"Cut me a thick steak off him." Collie Bill nodded to Slocum.

"I'll have the same thing."

"Potatoes, too?" Collie Bill asked.

"It comes with all the trimmings, bread, gravy, you name it, even dessert. Coffee?"

"Yes, ma'am."

Slocum didn't recognize anyone in the place and that made him grateful. She brought their coffee and promised them their steak was cooking. Then she went and flirted with a man in a ready-made brown suit. He acted like she was in heat and he was her answer. Slocum noted he left her a quarter tip after a private whisper in her ear when he stood up that she nodded her head in agreement to. Women must be in short supply in Pagosa.

The elk was good, the mashed potatoes were creamy, the gravy thick enough, and they had sourdough biscuits and real butter. They topped that off with apple pie and more hot coffee. Meal, tip, and all cost a dollar for the two of them, but it was worth it.

Collie Bill decided to go check out a bar or two, and Slocum said he was going to look at the river. Enough light shone from the main street business district to illuminate his way down to the shore of the swift stream. Clouds of fog rose off the hot springs that mixed with the cold air and river water. Kind of like Coulter's Hell when he broke off from the Lewis and Clark's main bunch and discovered Yellowstone. Slocum had read about that as a boy.

Later, Slocum had seen what Yellowstone was like, and could imagine being the first white man to find all that game with those mud pots and geysers. Wind swept the steam off the hot springs and across his face in a veil.

"Come on in. The water's great," a woman said, and he blinked at the sight of her white bare shoulders with her wet hair plastered down. She was bobbing neck-deep in the stream. She turned like a river otter and in the dim light, he saw her bare breast for a moment as she rolled out and swam a short distance. Then she came back.

"You can't get far out. It gets cold fast." Now she was up to her chin in the water. Obviously, she was standing on the bottom of the eddy.

"You swim all the time down here?"

"Whenever I get to Pagosa I do."

"Where do you live the rest of the time?" He squatted down on the edge and tossed pebbles into the water.

She wrinkled her nose. "Down in New Mexico. We've got a ranch down there."

"Any hot springs on it?"

"There's one. Shed your clothes. Ain't nobody else fool enough to come down here. But I've got to warn you, you'll freeze your butt off getting out."

"So?"

He looked around. There was no one in sight and she didn't look half bad. And she was out there tempting him—that's what he called a naked woman at night swimming in a river, inviting a total stranger to get in the water with her. So he shed his boots, coat, shirt, and pants. He was beginning to wonder if this was some trick or if he was crazy undressing in freezing weather. Too late now.

When he looked up, she was gone. Damn, she'd tricked him. He dove in, swam a ways, quickly discovered the cold side of the hole, and came back into the eddy fed by the thermal water. It was warm and it did feel good. Suddenly, she popped out of the water in his face, threw her arms around his neck, and stuck her hot tongue in his mouth.

Her hand was checking him out. He squeezed her hard against his body and felt her rock-hard breasts in his chest. For moment, he thought they'd both freeze, but she slipped down in the water and then led him to a deeper place.

"You ain't half bad." She slicked her short hair back from her face with both hands, then laughed at him. Mischief danced in her dark eyes. "I've coaxed a few drunk cowboys in a few times, and then I've scampered away and left them to freeze."

He reached out and pulled her to him. She pressed herself

against him and hugged him tight. She straddled his leg and rubbed her pubic patch on it until his erection began to poke her.

"Ever done it underwater before?" she asked.

"Sure, but never in a snowstorm." Big flakes had begun to fall, and soon her head was covered in a crown of white. She moved over, raised her left leg, and reached down to insert his hard dick in her gates while he steadied her, holding her firm waist.

"Whew, that feels wonderful." She put her face on his chest as if embarrassed, and hugged him. His hips began to move his throbbing rod in and out of her firm pussy. He could feel her clit growing hard as a nail, and she was arching her back for him. Their breath came like runaway racehorses, and her fingernails were clawing his back. Harder, faster, damn, he wished he had her in bed where he could really pound her ass. His head was swirling like the water around them and the snowflakes in the darkness that reflected some light. Then he came.

The surge from the bottom of his sac drew all his strength up and poured it into her. She collapsed in his arms and floated dreamily.

"What do they call you?" Slocum asked. It was snowing harder, and he worked them out into deeper water.

"May. May Booster. What's yours?"

"Tom White," he said, wondering where her brothers were at.

"Can I see you again?"

"Depends. Where will you be at?"

With both hands, she swept her wet hair back and upset the crown of snowflakes. "I can meet you at the cabin. Don't come to the ranch. My brothers hate anyone I like. The cabin is on Crow Creek. You take the trail west from Latimer's stage station. That's Crow Creek and the hot springs are five miles west. No one comes up there in the winter. Ah, sometimes an old Injun, but he won't bother us. Next full moon. Can you find it?"

"I'll try. Your cabin's there?"

"Yeah, we use it for a cow camp in the summer. Got a BB branded on the door."

"What about your brothers?"

"I've stayed up there for weeks before, they never came to

check on me. They don't care about me going up there. Think that I'm getting away from their bitching."

"Next full moon?"

"Yeah." She swung on his neck. "Hell, I'll be peeing in my pants by then for you, Tom White. You buy cattle?"

"Sometimes, when there's money in it."

She looked him hard in the eye. "You must think I'm some kinda cheap whore."

"Did I say that?"

"No, but you're thinking it. Jump in a river in a snowstorm and stick your pecker in a naked woman. She sounds like one to me."

He kissed her hard and felt her firm breast in his right hand. "A man don't kiss whores."

"Shit-fire, you're neat, Tom White. I hope to God you make it to Crow Creek." Then she captured him around the neck and put her face close to his. "I really mean it. I sure hope you can make it."

Her mouth was hungry and he enjoyed it. *They had a sister*.

"You married—" Then she waved her hand in front of his face. "Don't tell me, I don't want to know."

He leaned over and whispered in her cold ear, "No."

"What do you do? I mean for a living."

"Little as I can get by with."

"And I met you in a damn snowstorm, naked as a buck in a hot river." She shook her head in disbelief and pulled him toward the shore. "This is crazy."

Crazy would never explain it. He managed to get dressed between the blasts of snow and wind. He began shaking from the cold—May was already gone in the night and swirling flakes. Wrapped in his leather coat, he hurried to the livery a block away. There he hugged the potbellied coal stove in the bunkroom to drive the deep cold out of his body and dry his clothes before he climbed into the upper bed.

Collie Bill was already snoring in the lower one. A half hour later, Slocum still wasn't warm through and through. He shivered every few minutes and clenched his fist under the covers thinking about his arctic swim. May Booster was in her early twenties. Five feet six or more. Her body was hard as a rock. Belly muscled like a man's. She must do lots of physical ranch work—as wiry as she was. Hay stacking, shucking fodder, setting posts. He could recall her calloused hands going over his privates and brushing his face. Her breasts were firm and capped with hard nipples in the cold. The short-cut hair made it easy for her to care for it.

She was no house pet—next full moon on Crow Creek . . . He finally fell asleep.

"You fall in the river last night?" Collie Bill looked him in the eye from inches away standing beside the bed. There was a lamp on. The others in the stuffy room were coughing and grumbling as they woke up and began getting dressed.

"Come on, we're having breakfast with an old buddy," Collie Bill said.

"Who?"

"Carver Bledstone. You remember him?"

"Abilene or Newton, huh?" Slocum tried to recall the big man.

"He's still as powerful as ever."

"What's he doing up here?"

"Like the rest, looking to get rich."

"What's his plan?" Legs over the edge, Slocum bent over to pull on a boot. Damn, he felt hungover and depleted. She'd sure wrung all the strength out of him.

"You find a poker game up the street?" Collie Bill asked.

Was he asking did he poke her? "Yeah, it was all right. I broke even."

Amused, Slocum strained to pull on the other boot. Hints of the taste of May Booster's tongue were still in his mouth, along with the barefoot tracks of some army.

Carver roared like a grizzly at the sight of the two of them entering the café. The big red-bearded man rushed over to greet them. He gave Slocum a bear hug and a clap on the back. "Great to see you, amigo. My old compadre here, Bill, he told me that you were here."

"Question. Why is the great Bledstone here?"

"Have a seat. Have a seat. Hell, I figured there's still some country left up here to run a cow. Damn honyockers got the plains about covered and all plowed under. Have a seat, you two. Gal, bring them each a big breakfast," he said to the waitress. "They're cowboys and are liable to founder and die on your good cooking."

She poured coffee in mugs and agreed. Then she left with a swirl of her skirt. A little too much of an ample-bodied woman to catch Slocum's eye, but Collie Bill followed her retreat with interest.

"Tell me what you've found." Slocum straddled the chair and took a seat.

Bledstone lowered his voice. "Why, this country's got so many rustlers working it, you'd have to sleep with your damn cows."

"My opinion. They take cattle in a shakedown operation. Folks are too scared to even try to stop them. My ex-employer even refused my help to run them off for her."

"Her?"

"Señora Peralta."

"Oh, I met her once. Man, she's cold as a Montana blizzard." Bledstone looked around to be certain they were alone. "Tell me. Has she got as tight a pussy as I think it is?"

Slocum shook his head. "I ain't been closer than six feet of her."

Bledstone shook his head. "Hell, I got that close. Boy, she's the snow goddess, ain't she?"

"I figure so."

"Well, I don't feel so bad if the king hoss never got any closer than that to her."

"He didn't," Collie Bill testified. "Hell, we'd both liked to have tasted some of her tequila."

Slocum thought about her small shapely butt encased in those leather pants. It might be something to cup it in his hands and pound on her for a long time. He better stop wishing and go to eating. The waitress had delivered the platter of ham, eggs, and fried potatoes, a heaping plate of steaming biscuits, a dish of butter and one of blood-red chokecherry jam.

Bledstone excused himself to go talk to a man seated on a stool at the long bar.

Collie Bill winked at Slocum before he dove in to eat. "Wonder what old Bledstone has on his mind."

"We better inhale it so we can escape him."

"Right."

"I'm back. Boys, boys." He lowered his voice. "I figured you, me, and Slocum here could run a bunch of them varmints out of the country. I have a—man that will pay good money to get rid of them."

"Who's that?" Collie Bill asked, cutting his look around to be certain his words would not be overheard.

"Dan Thorpe."

Collie Bill whistled.

Slocum gave Bledstone a sharp nod. "He wants 'em dead. I've been on their team before. The only good stage robber is a dead one in their book."

"Dead or alive with evidence."

"What will he pay?" Slocum asked.

"He's hard up right now. Five hundred a head."

"Give me some names," Slocum said, between the salty sweet bite of ham and the hot biscuit.

"Kid Langtry, Ship Nelson, and—"

"One-Eye Davis?"

"How did you know him, Slocum?"

"We met them coming up here."

"They tough?"

Slocum shook his head. "But they're dangerous as a stick of blasting powder."

"How do we get them?"

"They're a couple of days' ride south hunkered down in this snow."

"That's fifteen hundred dollars for them three alone."

"Sounds easy," Collie Bill said, and went back to eating. When the waitress brought the coffeepot by for refills, they hushed, and once she was gone they began again.

"Who else?"

"You know the Booster brothers?" Bledstone asked.

"Cal and Rip?"

"Yeah. They've got the same reward tacked on them if we can tie them in on any robberies. Some black named Sims and five other guys work for them brothers."

"Who else?"

"Some bitch named Mary Murphy. Gambler, whore. Dresses in black. Kinda secretive."

"What did she do?"

"I guess she fucked the local agent out of two grand."

"Nobody pays two grand for a piece of ass." Slocum shook his head to keep Collie Bill out of it.

"Well, the more he lost at her table, the harder she fucked him that night after the game."

"She never stole that money, he did."

"Don't matter. The big man wants her hung out and dried. You know where she is?"

Slocum shook his head.

"Well, we can find her later."

Those big express companies did things like that. Slocum never missed the big boys they took out that had held up lots of stages, especially those that shot folks in the course of the crime, but the small-timers like Mary Murphy didn't deserve a death sentence. She'd never robbed anyone or any stage, or held a gun to that agent's head to get him to climb in the saddle. Maybe she'd told this big agent that his dick was too small about the time that he stuck it in her. Slocum about chuckled out loud over that thought. She'd've done that if the opportunity had slipped up on her.

"Well? You two in with me?" Bledstone wiped his mouth with the back of his hand and looked anxious for an answer.

"What do you think, Slocum?" Collie Bill asked.

"We were going to get rid of some rustlers. Guess they hold up stages, too."

"How did you aim to do that?" Bledstone asked.

"Tie a tin can on the scared ones' tails and send them packing. But for five hundred we can bring them in."

"With evidence," Bledstone reminded him.

"Hell, we'll get signed confessions out of 'em."

"Yeah," Collie Bill agreed. "Signed confessions."

Slocum wasn't going to tell him how they'd get them out of the wanted men until the time came. The man might get squeamish before then if Slocum did. Bledstone might be tough, but he wasn't ready for this deal; Slocum hoped Collie Bill would be by the time they got their first prisoner.

"Where do we start?" Bledstone asked. "Since you two know where some of them are at."

"We know where they were. Hell, they may be in Texas by now."

"Yeah, I savvy that, but at least we've got a lead."

"He fork over any money for expenses?' Slocum asked.

"You mean the Wells Fargo man?"

Slocum frowned in disgust at him. "Who else is going to give us diddly in this deal?"

"No, he said that five hundred a man was a handsome sum for those two-bit outlaws."

"Well, how much money you got?"

"Why—why?"

"'Cause it's snowing like a paper mill out there." Slocum indicated the outside. "We'll need a tent, a couple of packhorses. Supplies, horse feed, hell, he wants them, he can outfit us."

"I'd—I'll have to talk to him about that."

"Well, where is he?"

"At the ho-hotel. I'll meet you back here for—ah—dinner. Noontime."

"Get those things we need. I ain't freezing my ass off out there under a blanket and eating uncooked beans. Then we'll talk about riding out."

"I'll—I'll do that."

"Noontime, we'll be here waiting for the answer. Thanks for breakfast." Slocum reset the hat on his head, stood, and put on his leather coat. Buttoned up, he nodded to Bledstone. "Noon—here."

"Su-sure."

Out in the falling snow, Collie Bill elbowed him, looking up and down the street. "You ever hear Bledstone stutter like that before?"

"No, we had him in a corner. I ain't interested in no carrot on a stick that this Dan Thorpe has held out there. I want the expenses, too. It might take us months to find them guys with winter and snow covering this country. We need expenses anyway."

"So we're going to get paid to clean up this trash?" Collie Bill shook his head in disbelief.

"Looks that way."

"Not a bad deal," Collie Bill said. "Where you headed?"

"Telegraph office."

They moved over for a woman with a bundle in her arms to hurry past them.

"Who're you telegraphing?"

"Pete Olsen in Tombstone."

"Will he warn her?"

"If they don't find her out."

"Hell, that didn't sound fair anyway."

"I told you, they do it their way."

"If I could borrow ten on our future earnings, I'd go buy some wool underwear."

"Here's ten. But I expect Wells Fargo to foot the clothing bill."

"Thanks. A game of poker sounds warm and inviting." Collie Bill saluted him and was gone in the shifting flakes to cross the street.

At the Western Union, Slocum came in stomping off the wet snow and wrote the curt note to Pete Olsen, Big Horn Bar, Tombstone, Arizona Territory.

TELL MARY ABOUT THE EXPRESS POSTER SIGNED HER EX

He paid the key operator. It would have to do. Wells Fargo would keep an eye on all of them. In this case, it was all he dared. Maybe she'd slip away all wrapped up. He wrinkled his nose at the thought of her stinking so bad the last time they were together. He hoped she'd found a bath since then.

12

He was back in the livery barn, hoping to check over his saddle and girth and clean his .44. Poker didn't sound near as good as just loafing. Besides, he wanted to rest up. The days ahead would be severe when they were on the go and hard after those rannies.

He was headed through the aisle in the dark barn. The structure was creaking and groaning under the snow load. The sharp whang of the alfalfa hay in the mow and the horse piss burned his nostrils. Men's sharp voices made him stop, turn, and listen. Slocum decided to climb in the loft and see what they were up to. In seconds, he was upstairs and could hear them.

"—fucking snow anyway. What did you learn about that damn Wells Fargo man?"

"He's here trying to recruit bounty hunters." Neither of the men's voices sounded familiar to Slocum.

"He having any luck?"

"He's hired some Texan named Bleedsow."

"That sumbitch Carver Bledstone?"

"Yeah, that's who it is. You know him?"

"Yeah, from Dodge. He's a tough bastard. But we can handle him. Who else has he got?"

"Fuck if I know. That's all I could find out."

"Where's May at? She needs to take these supplies home."

"In this snow?"

"Hell, yes, get her ass down here. She's probably still in the sack at the hotel."

"But—"

"Then you go along with her and make sure she gets there."

"Aw, hell—"

"And you mess with her and I find out, I'll cut your pecker off with a rusty saw."

"Hey, Boss, I never touch her. I know how you are about her."

"I wish I had Sims here . . ." The voice of the Booster brother trailed off, and Slocum couldn't hear his next words. But he figured Bledstone's life was in jeopardy and Booster didn't need to know who was on Bledstone's team.

The two led out a team of big mules to harness into the aisle. It was cold in the loft waiting for them to finish. They talked mostly about the two whores they'd spent the night before with. One was called Dovie and the other Curly Ann. Slocum learned all about the attributes of the prostitutes.

"I like her little fat legs."

"She wrap them around you?"

"Yeah, and she spurred my ass when I got her going. Whew, that was the good part."

"Whoa, mule. Damn, you stupid peckerwood—" Booster was fighting with one of the walleyed mules who tried to pull away from him. "Whoa. Whoa."

As he lay belly-down in the loft, Slocum hoped the mule kicked Booster in the head and killed him. Through a crack in the floor he could see the wild antics of the braying, hoof-throwing animal and Booster on the end of the lead rope with his boot heels not planted to hold him.

"Get the chain twitch. Get the twitch," Booster began shouting. "This crazy sumbitch is going to get away."

His shouting rousted a swamper up in the tack room and he ran in to help. The mule knocked him aside into a pile of horse-shit and straw. Booster's man caught a stray kick. He was holding his shin and hobbling around moaning when the mule ran toward him and he had to scramble to save his butt.

At last, Booster got the rope wrapped around a barn post and held tight as the head-slinging mule had a fit on the far end. When he charged Booster, the man took up slack, and soon the mule's head was secured tight against the post. Braying and screaming, the mule proceeded to kick up so much dust, Slocum felt his coughing would soon be out of control.

At last, the swamper had a chain twitch wrapped tight around the mule's upper lip and the animal stood straddle-legged blowing rollers out his nose. Booster and his man were coughing and panting for air, bent over holding their knees.

"Oh, hell, that damn mule needs to be shot."

"No, I need him to haul that stuff up to the ranch."

"By Gawd, me and May can't hook him up by ourselves."

"Don't unharness him then."

"We won't, by Gawd."

"Just so you get these supplies to the ranch."

"You guys going to argue all day or harness him?" the swamper asked. "My arm's tired of holding this damn twitch."

"Udall, get a hold of that twitch."

"Here, old man, I can hold him."

In a few minutes, the mules were harnessed and led outside. Slocum listened. They hitched them in the snow to the ambulance with the bows and canvas over them; then Udall drove them off. Booster came back inside and saddled a horse. He settled his bill with the swamper and left. The old man closed the big door muttering to himself and went back in the tack room to his bed and warm stove.

Slocum finally eased himself out of the loft. On the floor, he brushed the hay off his coat and slipped outside into the falling flakes. He needed to find Collie Bill, and after that warn Bledstone. Booster might be out to kill him and Thorpe as well. Secondly, Slocum and Collie Bill couldn't be connected to either one—Booster had spies in Pagosa that would sure tell him all they knew.

Twenty minutes later, Slocum found Collie Bill in a dark back corner of the Last Miner Saloon with a dove in his lap and his arm underneath her dress to the elbow. His unseen hand was no doubt playing with her crotch. Her face was buried in his neck, her arms wrapped around him, and she was breathing hard, hunching her butt against his obviously probing finger.

Collie Bill opened his half-shut eyes and blinked at the sight of Slocum. "Something wrong?"

Startled, the dove glanced up at Slocum for a moment, then settled back into her pleasure.

"We need to talk," said Slocum.

Collie Bill removed his hand. She cupped his face and kissed him. He said, "Aw, I have to quit, baby, just when it was getting so good, too."

She slipped off his lap, straightened her hem out, and then gave Slocum a damn-you look.

"Here, darling," Collie Bill said, and paid her fifty cents. "I'll be back later."

She smiled for him and pushed her slightly bulged belly hard up against the table for him to feel her pussy. "See what you're missing, darling?"

"I see. I won't forget you."

"Be sure you don't." Swinging her hips, she stalked away with several customers making catcalls after her as she crossed the room.

"Ah, that was Lucia. What do you need?"

"I just learned that Bledstone may be in big trouble. At the stables a few minutes ago, I heard one of the Booster brothers and his man Udall talking. Booster knows Wells Fargo has hired Bledstone. He also knows Thorpe is in town. But he doesn't know about us—yet."

"So he better not find out, right?"

"Right. Or our cover will be gone."

"Who told him? I wonder."

"Whores, bartender, snitches, hell only knows. Sims ain't here, which Booster hates, but he might do something on his own. Can you get word to warn Bledstone and not get detected?"

"Sure thing. Where will you be?" Collie Bill asked.

"At the café for supper. Meet you there about dark."

"Couple of hours, huh? Still snowing, isn't it?" Collie Bill nodded to indicate the two customers who had just come in the front doors mantled in white.

"It may get asshole-deep on a tall mule." Slocum chuckled privately.

"It damn sure might."

He could only imagine the trip May faced getting back to their ranch. Even tough men might have trouble in this blizzard. What was so important about getting those supplies back that it couldn't wait? Damned if he knew. And where was the big mulatto Sims at? Probably up to no good.

He went back to the livery and took a nap on his bunk, figuring he might miss some sleep that evening. The place stank of sweat, cigar smoke, and horse shit, but he wrinkled his nose and with his six-gun beside him under the covers on the cob-filled mattress, fell asleep. He awoke later at the cussing of someone coming in. Damn. He swung his leg over the side and mopped his face in his hands—a man couldn't even sleep without being disturbed. It was probably time to get up anyway.

"Fucking snow," the bearded newcomer swore, and held his hands toward the stove. A puddle was beginning around his blanket-wrapped feet.

"That would be a damn cold deal," Slocum said and laughed.

"Hell, I've still got to get over to Durango."

"You may be a day or so getting over there."

"Yeah, I may."

Slocum put on his felt hat and leather coat. "Good luck."

It was getting to be dark, the falling snow was lighter, but there were six to eight inches on the ground. It was a slushy muddy mess in the street he crossed—he figured that the road south would be like that for May. Might take two teams of wild mules to get her home. And would she be at that cabin for the full moon? Only time would tell.

He took a table in the back of the café and waited for Collie Bill. No telling how late he'd be, so Slocum sipped coffee the waitress brought by and poured for him. In a half hour, Collie Bill came in, saw him, and lumbered back there under his snow-splattered wool coat.

"I got it all straight. We can get whatever we need at Hall's Mercantile." He shed his coat and hung it on a wall peg, then straddled his chair to sit down. He lowered his voice. "They can't trace our account. The whole deal scared Bledstone, me telling him what we knew."

"What did he think we were after, dummies? These guys've been outwitting the law for years in Colorado and New Mexico. Get cross with them and your life ain't worth ten cents up here." Slocum shook his head in disgust.

"We can go get our underwear and what we need—anytime—" Collie Bill paused for the waitress. "You still got some of that fresh elk?"

"Yes."

"I'll have that."

"Me, too," Slocum said.

"I'll put the order in and bring you boys some coffee."

Slocum noticed how Collie Bill followed her retreat to the kitchen. She had too soggy a figure for him get an erection over very easily. "So Thorpe is providing us what we need?"

"Yeah. He wants that gang with One-Eye brought in first."

"No, you don't savvy how Wells Fargo thinks. They want them dead."

"Whatever they want, the world wouldn't cry over that loss."

Slocum drummed his fingers on the table. Two weeks till the full moon. Why then? Hell, he'd have to figure it out. She might perish in the damn storm on the road. No telling. Stranger yet, he hadn't seen her again. Pagosa wasn't that big of a place.

"You ain't said much." Collie Bill frowned at him.

"You did good. They're warned and we can get our supplies."

"We ain't leaving till after this snow lets up, are we?'

Slocum looked at him through the vapors off his coffee. "I damn sure ain't going anywhere."

"Good," Collie Bill said, and straightened up so the waitress could put his heaping patter of meat and potatoes before him.

"That enough food?" she asked him, standing back and sweeping the brown hair back from her face.

"I could always use a little more." He winked at her.

"I get off at nine. Back door," she said quietly.

"See you then. Mighty fine."

She gave a see-there look to Slocum and put his full plate down. He winked at her and then he thanked her. Obviously, both servings were larger than the night before.

Then, with his fork in hand, Collie Bill asked him, "What do you think?"

"Hell, I don't know. We've still got time to get that underwear on the tab."

"I'll damn sure get it, too. I'm tired of shivering."

They both laughed, and then got busy eating.

Later in the mercantile, they picked out woolen long handles, and they also charged a new wool shirt apiece to the account. When they left the store with their bundles under their arms, the snow had quit and a thousand stars dotted the sky.

"Maybe it's going to break off," Collie Bill said.

"Don't hock your long handles. It'll be colder than blue blazes before morning without any cloud cover."

"Depends how cold it gets, I may stay all night." He grinned.

Slocum nodded and they parted. Back in the livery bunk, he couldn't get May Booster off his mind or his dick either. How was she making it with those wild mules and deep snow? Damn, he'd've loved to get her where he could have really poked it to her.

Why was her brother staying in Pagosa and sending her home? There were a million unanswered questions in this deal. Why was One-Eye so important to Wells Fargo that they wanted him and his gang brought in first? Maybe in two weeks he'd learn more from May Booster.

13

After a frigid sunrise, the weather broke, temperatures rose above freezing, and the snow began to melt. They loaded a packhorse with supplies and headed south, planning to meet Bledstone at the Flores stage stop. Slocum trusted Flores. Besides, Flores's wife Juanita was a great cook and good company. By mid-morning, the solar heat was enough to keep Slocum and Collie Bill warm in the new long handles and woolen shirts, and they could unbutton their coats.

Though a cool south wind swept over the snow cover, Slocum enjoyed the respite from the storm. He and Collie Bill rode stirrup to stirrup down the forest-lined road with virgin timber towering on both sides. By evening, they'd made Wall's stage stop. After a meal of white beans and venison, Wall told them they could sleep in a shed attached to the main structure. The tobacco-spitting old man had a young Ute breed wife he called Girl, and her dark slanted eyes kept sneaking looks at him and Collie Bill behind the old man's back.

She stood about four feet six and wasn't bigger than anything, but she worked. Dressed in deerskin-fringed clothing with lots of beads sewn on the front, and with a belt of hammered silver dollars around her waist, she cut a nice small figure moving around the room serving them. But Slocum knew Girl wanted more than the two bits she charged them for their supper.

Her high cheekbones left her face too long to be pretty, but she had a rich brown coloration. The slender nose had been broken at least once. The way she whirled around and stayed busy made him admire her.

When Wall and Girl were out of the room, Collie Bill looked over his coffee cup and grinned. "Bet she's a damn sight tighter than Madge was."

"Madge wasn't tight?"

Collie Bill glanced at the doorway and then shook his head. "Loose as a goose. But she was warm to sleep with."

"That counted for something."

"Yeah, but I should have gone and found Lucia instead." Collie Bill shook his head in defeat. "Now, that gal had a real bear trap. But I figured by the time I found her again, I'd be the sixth one that night."

Slocum chuckled. He was probably right.

Everyone turned in after the meal. The old man showed them the shed on the side. There were some bunks for them. Wind came in through several un-chinked cracks between the small logs, but for Slocum's part, the add-on shack beat sleeping in the wet snow. He soon fell asleep, and awoke when he felt a silencing finger pressed to his lips.

His fist closed around the Colt grips in the bed beside him. And in the near darkness, he could make out her long braids hanging down. He threw back the cover and moved over. She wore a too-large nightshirt that hung to her knees, and she jumped back when he raised the revolver to put it on the crate beside the bed. When the gun was set aside, he pulled her toward him and she relaxed some. She acted like the whole thing was new to her and she'd needed lots of courage to even wake him. Good actress or not, he wasn't certain, but she did not stink of bear grease, and might have had a recent bath since she didn't have a musky smell. She snuggled against him on her side and put both hands under her head.

He undid the buttons on her shirt from the bottom up. She didn't act upset, nor did she act anxious for him to hurry. When he finished, he pushed the shirt off her shoulders and felt her warm smooth skin. With his thumb pad, he rubbed on her left nipple until it popped alive. Her breath began to come faster. Then she hugged him to make him stop.

With his fist under her chin, he drew her up on top of him until he could raise his head up and kiss her lips. She drew back afterward, and in the dim starlight coming in a small window, he saw the mixed emotions written on the face of an Indian woman who'd been kissed for the first time. As she sprawled on top of him, her skin felt warm against his. Her small knee in his crotch nudged his privates. He reset his blankets to cover them, and then cupped her firm small butt in his hands and they kissed again. This time, he sought her tongue and she responded.

Soon, she spread her short legs apart and reached under to insert him. The gates were tight and his swollen erection large, but she kept pumping it in deeper and deeper. While he enjoyed her, he really wanted her underneath him. He raised her up and she frowned in the silver light, but obeyed.

Soon she was on her back with him on top. He threaded his hard dick into her wet gates. A small "Oh" escaped her lips when he passed through her tight ring. Her back arched and she pulled him down on top of her. They went and went, trying to control their gulping of air, until at last he came deep inside her and she pressed her hips to him for all of it.

Side by side, they huddled on the cot. He was about to go to sleep when she slid down, pulling on his half-deflated dick with her small hands. Her lips soon closed around it, and the hard roof of her mouth rubbed the head so hard, he felt his hard-on swell up to even larger proportions.

He clutched her head as she grew wilder and wilder. His hips ached to plunge it into her. His butt rose up with each deep movement she made. Then, from the action of the edge of her small teeth and her hand cuddling his sac, he came, and she raised up from under the blanket tent with white cum trailing out the right side of her grin.

With the back of her hand, she wiped at it, and then crawled up to whisper in his ear, "You fuckee me one more."

He scratched his sac, then felt his depleted testicles and closed his eyes. Was there any more in them? He rose up and, like a river otter, she slipped under him.

He had the stiffening dick in his hand ready to insert it in her when he began to hear the hard coughing coming from the station. It was the old man. Like a fleeting shadow, she slipped out of bed and put the white shirt on while going out the door. More coughing, and Slocum listened hard for any words. There were none, and things went silent again save for the creaking of the old building. He finally fell asleep again.

In the darkness, he woke and heard the sound of pots and pans. She was up out there, getting food ready. He got out of his bunk and shook Collie Bill. "We need to shake a leg."

"Coming, pard." He lowered his voice as he threw his stocking feet over the side. "Was it tight as I said?"

Slocum nodded.

"Good." Then he chuckled. "That old man ain't worn it out, that's for sure."

They dressed—then pulled their boots on and stomped out of the shed. Slocum went to the kitchen side door and saw her busy at the iron stove frying corn mush.

"He around?" he asked in a soft voice.

"Him get horses ready. Stage come soon."

Slocum nodded. "You all right?"

"Me fine. You leave today?"

"We got to get down in New Mexico on business."

With a confident grin on her coffee-colored face, she turned from her cooking to look him up and down. "You come back. We fuck big-time. All night."

"I'll remember that."

She nodded in approval and turned back to the sizzling mush. "Girl be here then."

"Yes, ma'am."

After breakfast, the stage still hadn't arrived. Slocum paid the man forty cents for their food and lodging. He offered them a swig of his corn liquor from a crock jug, but they declined and went to saddle and pack their horses.

"Even whiskey might not kill the germs that old man has." Collie Bill scowled across the white staging area at the building. He jerked his latigo tight and threaded it through the ring. "Consumption. He's coughing up his rotten lungs in bits and pieces."

"Yeah, he's got it and bad." Slocum was satisfied with the diamond hitch on the packhorse, but his feet were cold from stomping around in the wet snow.

In the saddle at last, they rode out. The brown vixen had never made eye contact with him.

"Stage must have got stopped somewhere south of here," Collie Bill said in his saddle.

"Yes, it might have." He was thinking more about May Booster and her mules than the stage. Had she made it? The old man had never mentioned her passing, but the wagon tracks went by there. He'd noted them the day before, halfway expecting to run into her on the road. Maybe she'd made it fine.

The brown vixen back there acted like she was ready for another round. He wanted to laugh about her unexpected escapades with him in the bed, but instead, he kept the whole matter to himself and rode on.

In mid-morning, they came over a rise and he smelled wood smoke. He could see someone around the fire built at the edge of the road. He thought there was a stage wheel sticking up on the lower side of the road.

"They have a wreck?" Collie Bill asked, reining up his horse.

"Looks like it."

They rode on to the fire. The driver was holding his hands out to the fire's heat. The coach was over on its side and almost upside down. A dead horse in harness lay on the ground with the broken tongue.

"What happened here?" Collie Bill asked.

"A mountain lion spooked 'im," the whiskered man said with a disgusted shake of his head. "I sent for help. Some gal in a wagon came by here a couple of hours ago. She's going to telegraph it in."

"Everyone all right?" Slocum asked, dismounting.

"I sent the only passenger I had back with her. Poor old boy broke his arm. Maybe more. Hell, there ain't no medical doctor short of Española or Pagosa Springs. Figured he might get a ride on down there. My name's Byran."

He stuck out a hand.

"Slocum. That's Collie Bill. You want a ride out of here?"

"Nice to meetcha. Naw, I'll have to stay here until they send another coach. I've got mail and shipments to look after."

"A man could get damn cold up here before they get up here." Collie Bill led his roan across the snowy ruts to look closely at the upset stage.

"It's my job," Byran said, spitting black tobacco juice on the melting white stuff. He wiped his mouth on the back of his hand. "Sure gets to be a damn tough job. Holdups, snow and ice, colder than blazes." He drew in a deep breath until his shoulders shuddered under his heavy wool coat.

Slocum nodded. "Hate to leave you to freeze up here."

"Go on. I'll be fine."

Slocum and Collie Bill remounted and rode on.

"Wonder who the gal with the wagon was that was out in this kind of weather and conditions. Must be a tough ole heifer." Collie Bill shook his head, and they trotted south toward the sun, which had warmed as the day progressed.

"Must be," Slocum answered. He wanted to smile at his words, recalling the strong sulfurous vapors swirling around his head in the snowflakes and beneath the swirling surface with him hunching it to her tight core. *Yes, she must be.*

Trotting their horses to gain time, at this rate Slocum expected they'd overtake the wagon in a few hours. Collie Bill could see the "old heifer" for himself. He might change his opinion of her. With the rising temperature, Slocum opened his jacket more. They were coming down a long grade when Slocum caught first sight of the tarped-down rig ahead. He could only see one person on the seat driving, and wondered where the passenger was riding.

"That must be her," Collie Bill said.

"Must be."

She sawed her mules to a stop when they drew alongside her, and then she nodded at them. "Howdy, gents."

"Good day, ma'am," Slocum said and took off his hat. "You still have the passenger that was hurt?"

She tied off her reins on the brake pole. "If he's still alive, he's in the back under the tarp. He was sure bad battered up from that wreck."

Collie Bill slipped off his horse and scowled. "Byran said he had a broken arm."

"He didn't tell you the rest of the poor man's problems?"

"No, he didn't."

She jumped down and strode to the back of the wagon in her knee-high black boots. Over her britches, she wore a full skirt and a long black woolen coat, with a blue silk rag tied around her throat. By this time Slocum figured his partner, by the look on his face, had changed his mind about the sparkling blue-eyed "heifer."

Slocum dismounted and watched her undo the tarp tie-downs, and then Collie Bill flipped the tarp up.

From his higher vantage point, Slocum could see someone tucked under several blankets in a space that had been made between barrels and crates. The injured person never moved. He must have been hard for Collie Bill to see standing on the ground, and the cowboy scrambled up into the wagon.

"You sleeping?" he asked, kneeling down in the box between all the items on the wagon.

No answer.

"Is he dead?" she asked, standing on her toes but lacking the height to see over the tailgate.

Collie Bill bent over and then straightened up with a wary headshake. "He ain't breathing."

"We did all we could for him," she said, jerking off her thin leather driving gloves and looking disappointed at the mushy snow. "Me and that driver—all I wanted to do was—"

"Sure wasn't your fault, ma'am."

"My name's May."

Then Collie Bill asked her the question burning a hole in Slocum. "You alone out here, May?"

"You can see my help." She made a sweep around with her hands. "What do we do now?"

"Roll him up in a blanket and drop him off at the next stage stop," Slocum said, walking up leading Heck. Where was Udall? He was supposed to go along with her.

Collie Bill took out the dead man's wallet, went through it, shaking open a small letter and reading it to himself, and then waved a wad of folding money he'd discovered in it. "Wow. He must have sold the ranch. This letter says his name is Gunther Gauge. Lives at Mason, Texas."

"Don't sound German enough for me," Slocum said, amused at his own thought about the man's origin.

She blinked at Slocum. "What does that mean, Tom?"

He caught Collie Bill's reaction to her calling him *Tom*. He'd never said his real name to her, and the Tom part must have jarred his buddy.

"Aw, that western Texas hill country is full of the Hauns and Heinrichs. Gauge ain't German enough."

She nodded and turned back to Collie Bill. "Do I need to help roll him up?"

Colllie Bill shook his head. "I can do it. I'll stuff this money and his wallet back in his coat."

"Fine, I guess they will send all that back to his heirs." She undid her coat and opened it. Hands on her hips, she stood waiting. It exposed the .30-caliber Colt and holster she wore on her waist. Also showed off the shape of her breasts under the man's shirt she wore.

"In a country like this—why ain't a pretty girl like you found a man to help you?" Collie Bill asked, busy preparing the body.

"You'll have to ask my brothers that question."

"They won't let you?"

"You have that right."

"What's your brothers' names?" He was busy securing the corpse in a gray blanket.

"Booster, Cal and Rip."

He blinked at her words in disbelief.

"You know them?"

"No, ma'am."

"We can leave him at the next stage station," Slocum said.

"I won't miss him," she said with a scowl. "Wasn't nothing I could do for him. I just wanted to try to get him to help."

"No one's blaming you."

"Well, I sure ain't no doctor," she said, downcast.

Slocum hugged her shoulder, realizing how hard she was taking the man's death. "We better get moving."

He and Collie Bill tied down the tarp. Slocum waved her toward the seat, and watched her step up and settle on it almost effortlessly. She unwound the reins, stomped off the brake, and spoke sharply to the mules, holding them back as the wagon began to roll.

Slocum swung in the saddle and Collie Bill rode over. "Where did you meet her, *Tom*?"

"Pagosa."

Collie Bill nodded as if satisfied, and they set their ponies in a long trot after her.

The snow had begun to melt and water dripped off the rocks and hills, turning the road into a mushy mess. Slocum wondered about Udall and where he'd gone—according to what Slocum knew, he was supposed to go along with her. Had he joined Cal to go after Bledstone?

Collie Bill had warned Bledstone that Booster or one of his bunch might try to kill him. Bledstone had told Collie that Thorpe wanted One-Eye Davis stopped more than the Boosters and that Slocum and Collie needed to capture One-Eye's gang first. They were the worst stage robbers in the territory. Bledstone was to join them at Española in a few days.

Slocum still had the planned meeting with May on his mind. He shed his coat in the warming sum. In the saddle, he turned and looked over his shoulder. Nothing.

"I'm going to ride with her on the seat for a while," he said to Collie Bill. "I might learn something."

Collie Bill agreed. "I'll take care of the buckskin."

Slocum nodded, and loped Heck up beside her. She looked a little surprised at his appearance, then began to grin as he stood up on the saddle, bounded over to the side of the wagon box, and caught the spring seat. He stepped in, and she scooted over to make room for him.

"Figured you needed a little company." He sat down beside her and slipped his arm around her shoulders.

"I can always use company. Especially you."

With a sly smile for him, she turned back to driving her mules. Collie Bill rode up, caught Heck by the bridle, and waved to them, settling into riding behind them. Four iron rims cut the slop, flinging some of it in a spray from each. The harness chains jingled to the mules' hard clop of hooves in the melting mess. Warm sun and her company against him settled Slocum on the seat.

"Where are you two going?" she asked.

"Española, to look for a man."

"Who?" She cut her blue eyes around at him.

"Ike Taylor, he owes Collie Bill some money," he lied. She might know One-Eye and that would be a mess. A sister to outlaws knew more outlaws than ordinary folks. They usually met each other over the course of time and mixed in social ways. So Ike Taylor would have to do. Besides, Ike was buried below the Canadian in the Nation.

"You still aiming to keep your word?" She cut a look at him.

"Why wouldn't I?"

"Oh, a big man like you could have any *puta* in Española. Why would he want to ride that far for some tomboy?"

" 'Cause she invited me?"

She shook her head like she wanted to clear it. "You've got a way of twisting things around, like kissing me and then telling me you don't kiss whores."

"I don't."

She gave his knee a shove with hers and turned forward, driving her mules. "We should be at Kitchner's station in a couple of hours," she said.

"How far you plan on going today?"

"The hay bottoms. That's where I turn west to the ranch."

"How far is it from there?"

"A good day's drive."

"Us being along with you isn't going to cause you any trouble with your brothers?"

"Nice of you to ask." She wrinkled her nose. "Some snitch might tell 'em."

"We can ride behind if we need to."

She looked over at him and blinked her blue eyes. "You're serious?"

Distracted by a red wing hawk's screams, Slocum used his hand to shade his eyes to see the bird. "I'm very serious."

"They just nag at me is all."

"About what?"

"How I need to find a rich man to marry."

"And?"

She laughed aloud. "What rich man would want me? I am not exactly a virgin."

"Don't tell him. He'll be so excited he'll never know."

She reined the mules up to ford a clear stream that meandered over the road. "Looks shallow enough."

"It's fine." He twisted to look back for Collie Bill—he was coming with Heck and the packhorse in tow.

"Get up!" Ready to go, she slapped the mules with the lines and they stepped gingerly into the water. Then they high-stepped and splashed across it. "You're new to this country, ain't ya?"

"Yes."

"Well, I better tell you, us Boosters ain't got a good reputation."

"You don't?"

"That's right. But we're cattlemen, that's all. Lots of what they say about us are flat lies."

"I wouldn't know or care."

"Good. You ever been married?"

"Nope."

"I don't figure you'd cotton to being home every night."

"You're probably right."

"Oh—" She glanced aside at him for a second. "I knew the night I seen you that you were a butterfly cowboy."

"Butterfly?"

"Yeah, flitting from flower to flower." Then she laughed out loud. "See how dumb I am?"

He squeezed her shoulder. May Booster was her own woman. Did she really believe they were only cattlemen?

They reached Hay Flats in mid-afternoon. She told Slocum she was satisfied and could push west to the ranch in the morning. They helped her unhook the mules. She was concerned about reharnessing them in the morning.

"We can harness them, ma'am," Collie Bill assured her.

Satisfied, she hiked off in the junipers to relieve herself.

"Learn anything today?" Collie Bill asked, putting up his harness on the wagon tongue.

"Not really. She says her brothers are only cattlemen, not outlaws."

"Reckon she really believes that?"

Slocum laid his gear out. "Damned if I know. We know what they're doing and have done or are accused of."

"Hell, she's a damn good distraction." They both laughed.

At sundown, May fried up some thin-sliced venison meat and boiled some rice with skillet flour gravy. They ate her mouth-watering food, seated around on a tarp, and watched a north-bound stage rush by on the main road.

"I hope we can hitch up those durn mules in the morning," she said, acting concerned.

With his mouth full, Slocum nodded until he could swallow. "We can handle that."

"I'll miss you two tomorrow."

"Is it a rough trip back into the ranch?" Collie Bill asked.

"It ain't an easy road in a wagon, but with the snow melting I'll make it," she said. "But I'll still miss the company."

"We could ride along for a ways," Slocum offered.

"Naw, you two have got business in Española collecting that money. Why, he might clear the country. You can't ever tell."

Slocum agreed and so did his partner, like he was in on the deal.

After supper, May washed the tin plates and Slocum dried them. Collie Bill conveniently turned in. Slocum led her with a bedroll under his arm uphill a ways under the stars. Making small talk, they soon had the bedroll unfurled and she began to undress. They stood on the top of it, with the canvas side under it to hold out the moisture. He toed off his boots, put his gun belt on the cedar bough, and then shed his pants. When he straightened, she stood naked before him, unbuttoning his underwear with fumbling fingers and a quick breath.

"Oh, I thought I'd have to wait weeks for this. I'm so excited I'm shaking."

"You didn't get all you wanted in the river?"

She drove a soft fist into his hard belly. "By no means. But it was as nice as it could have been."

Their bare skin was swept by the cool night wind, and they weren't long getting under the covers. She spread her legs out and nosed his half-hard erection into her. Then she raised her legs on both sides of him and pulled him down on top of her. "Make me scream."

His aching hips had that intent. His erection soon was filling her and she gasped, "Yes. Yes, I knew it was going to be great."

He buried it to the hilt in her pussy and she clutched him. "Stay."

With her hips in charge, she began to rock on her back, and he felt her swelling inside as she worked him over pulling hard on the sore head of his dick. Her efforts grew wilder and wilder, until at last she came and fainted underneath him.

Slowly, she began to stir as he worked in and out of her.

"Oh, my Gawd, I fainted," she mumbled, and tossed her head.

"Ever do that before?" he asked, braced over her and gently pumping his rod through her tight ring.

"No. Whew, I'm crazy."

"Hang on, you ain't through yet."

In minutes, he had her breathing harder than a freight train on a steep grade. Her hands clutched his upper arms to hang on as she met his every thrust. Penetrating her with his fiery swollen rod, he was working up a real storm when he finally came. She followed suit, and they collapsed in each other's arms.

There wasn't much sleeping that night in his bedroll. In the cold predawn, he washed his face with a handful of snow and then dressed, groggy, sore, and went off to start a cooking fire for her.

Slocum and Collie Bill hitched the mules while she stirred up some food and coffee. Then they packed and saddled their own horses, so by the time the first peach sky lit up the saw-toothed eastern horizon, everything was ready to roll, and they ate their meal squatted on their boot heels.

"Man, I could sure use you two every trip," she said. "You two can really handle those mules."

"We get along."

"Hope you two collect that money."

"We will, little lady," Collier Bill said, and went to refill his plate.

"In ten days?" she asked Slocum under her breath.

"I'll do my damnedest."

"That's enough." And she smiled.

With Gauge's blanket-wrapped body tied down over the packhorse, they waved good-bye and she drove her mules west. Slocum watched her disappear in the junipers, and swung in the saddle.

"I'm surprised you can still walk," Collie Bill teased.

Slocum leaned back in the saddle against his stiff back. "It is a miracle."

14

Slocum and Collie Bill reached Flores Station by afternoon. Manuel was nowhere in sight, and Juanita rushed out and stared at the sight. "You two return, I see. Who is the dead one?" She frowned at the sight of it.

"Man named Gauge from Texas," Collie Bill said, and swung off his roan. "The stage wrecked up north near the Colorado line. A woman was trying to get him to medical help and he died. We figured the stage folks would send his things on to his kin in Texas."

"They ought to. Guess we better bury him."

"Lead us to the shovels," Slocum said, and looked around. "Your husband isn't here?"

"No, he went to help them get the wrecked stage. You didn't see him on the road?" A worried frown wrinkled her smooth forehead.

"When did he go up there?" Collie Bill asked.

"Yesterday evening, he rode his bay horse up there and said he'd be back in a day."

"He could have rode by our camp while we were asleep. We spent last night at the hay flats."

She gave a worried look to the north, then gathered her skirts and nodded at them. "Come on in. I can tell you haven't eaten much since you left here the other day."

"You run this by yourself?" Collie Bill asked.

"I can. He's had to be gone before. I'm fine."

"Any word from Perla? I mean Señora Peralta?" Slocum asked, pouring himself a cup of coffee while she scurried about getting food ready to cook.

She stopped in the side door and looked back at them. "She is fine as far as I know."

"Good," Slocum said, and noted how Juanita acted on edge. "I just wondered about her."

In minutes, Juanita returned with some large slabs of red meat in her hands. It looked like elk to him. "Manuel shot a nice one the day you left. I cut off two big steaks."

"You're going to spoil us," Collie Bill said, straddling a ladder-back chair and setting his tin coffee cup on the table.

"You both need spoiling. Just sit down, food's coming." She stoked the range's firebox and wiped her forehead on the back of her hand. "It'll be ready in a jiffy."

"No rush. We can bury Gauge after we eat."

"Was he kinda balding and wore a suit?" she asked.

"That's him. Guess he ate here that night?" Collie Bill said.

"Yes. He was a nice man. I'm sorry he's dead."

"You need any horses harnessed or got ready?" Collie Bill asked her.

"Not till nine o'clock tonight. There's a stage going south then." She chewed on her lower lip. "Maybe they will have seen Manuel on the road."

"I'm sure that he's fine," Collie Bill said to reassure her.

"I hope so."

They ate her large steaks, fried onions, and potatoes from her cellar along with sliced sourdough bread and butter. Slocum felt too full to dig a grave, but after the meal they both went up on a rise where she told them to bury Gauge, and began shoveling dirt.

The wind came down out of the north and some clouds appeared before sundown. They finished the grave in the twilight, and she brought a lamp up for them to see by. Slocum went down in the grave and Collie Bill handed him the body.

"The money—" he said, and lowered the light down to Slocum.

"I'd forgotten all about it," Slocum said, working in the narrow grave with loose dirt crumbling in on him as he moved around to untie the ropes. At last, he had the wallet and money out of the man's suit coat. He handed it up to Collie Bill.

"You won't mind pulling off his boots?" Collie asked.

Slocum had had all the dead body he wanted, not to mention sharing the hole with the body. But he agreed.

"I just wondered," said Collie Bill. "Some men store their money in their boots."

It was difficult to get to his footwear, but when Slocum pulled off the first shoe, paper money showered down.

"Look at it," Collie Bill said. "Where did he get all that new money?"

Standing straddling the corpse, Slocum passed handfuls of currency up. Both Collie Bill and Juanita were taking the money he handed to them. When he was satisfied he'd gotten all of it, he removed the second boot and more money showered down.

"What are you thinking?" Collie Bill asked.

"We came close to burying a fortune." Slocum laughed and bent over to pick up more. He wished the man had left some word about next of kin, but he'd never had a chance. When all the money and the lantern were at last handed up, he let Collie Bill pull him out of the hole. Back on top, with his hands on his hips, he straightened his stiff back.

"How much is there?" he asked Juanita, who was sorting it in the lantern light.

"A couple thousand, I'd say."

"Is it real?" he asked, holding two bills up to the light.

"Feels real."

"There are good counterfeiters." He looked at the details on the bills.

"You think it is phony money?"

"If it is, it's really good. But folks take counterfeit money and go all over the country cashing it in and getting real money back in change."

They began to shovel dirt in the grave. On her knees, she was busy stacking the bills and counting the piles held down by small rocks in the lamplight. The grave was three-quarters completed when she announced the total as 918 dollars.

"Wonder where he got it," Collie said.

"We may never know."

"He might not have any kin."

"What then?" she asked.

"I guess we'd be the finders and get to keep it."

Collie Bill stopped shoveling. "You saying we should telegram that sheriff and ask if he has any heirs in Texas?"

"That's an idea." Slocum looked at stars and noted the clouds were moving in. Probably snow again in the next twenty-four hours.

They finished the grave and Slocum said a few words; then they walked back to the stage building. The lamps inside were shedding yellow light out the small windows.

"Which horses do we need to get ready?" Collie Bill asked her.

"Let's get our coats first, it's really turning colder, and then I'll show you. But really, I can do it by myself."

"No way," Slocum said. "You cook and we can harness the horses."

All three laughed as they headed for the front porch. Inside, she placed the money in a desk drawer for safekeeping, and they put on their coats. Outside, Juanita stood on the corral fence holding up the light, and showed them the horses to catch. When the horses were caught and harnessed, they were tied to a rack. And the three went back to the house.

She busied herself making meals for the next passengers to arrive, and served Slocum and Collie Bull two large pieces of huckleberry pie. Both men took their time cutting off small pieces with the sides of their forks and eating the tart sweet delicacy one dab at a time.

"I'd say this is as close to heaven as a man can get," Collie Bill said.

"Enjoy it. You two sure earned it," she said, putting on a

wrap and getting ready to slip outdoors. "I'm just checking on the stage." She looked up at the clock on the wall. "It's thirty minutes late."

Slocum nodded. "I'm sure it will get here."

But she was already outside and had closed the door.

"Juanita's sure nervous about everything tonight, isn't she?" Collie Bill considered the last of his pie. "I may lick this plate clean."

"First, over us not seeing her man on the road, and then, the stage was due here at nine and it's nine-thirty."

"I ain't figured that either about Manuel. If he rode up there to the wreck, he went right by us."

"Probably when we were sleeping." Slocum cradled the cup of coffee in his hands.

"I didn't figure you slept much last night."

"I wasn't looking for no rider on the road up there in the junipers."

They both laughed.

Juanita came back inside. "It's snowing."

"Came early," Slocum said, seeing the flakes melting on her shawl. "I thought it would be another day before it arrived."

She opened the potbellied stove and tossed in some split wood. "That should hold it for a while. Sure taking lots of wood."

The door burst open and the mulatto's dark face pushed inside. "Señora, come out here!"

Slocum's hand went for his gun butt. Collie Bill was on his feet. "What for?"

"It's her man." Sims turned in the open doorway and waved to someone outside. "You two bring him in."

"What has happened to him?" Her face was washed of color as she rushed toward the doorway.

"Collie Bill, stop her," Slocum said. "They're bringing him in."

She gasped at his words. "Bringing him in? What's happened to him?"

"Go easy," Collie Bill said, standing in her way.

"My poor Manuel—what happened to him?" She was wringing her hands and then holding her fists to her mouth. "Oh, no."

"We's don't know, lady," Sims said. "He must have been thrown off his horse. We found him beside the road and no sign of his horse. His neck, I think, was broken."

"Oh, no!" Hysterical, she let her flood of tears break loose.

Two men carried Manuel's limp body in the front door. Slocum directed them to the rear of the house and the sleeping room. Collie Bill tried to comfort her as they followed the men with the body.

"Where did you find him?" Slocum asked Sims.

"On the stage road about dark. Oh, ten miles north."

"Past the hay flats?"

"Yeah, way north of there, why?"

"He'd gone to help with the wrecked stage."

"We heard they wrecked one up there and some guy died in the wreck."

Slocum nodded. "We buried him."

Sims folded his arms over his barrel chest as if appraising Slocum. "You's pretty handy showing up all over, ain't you?"

"What are you getting at?" Slocum met his hard gaze. Sims's two men came out of the side room. Neither of them looked particularly tough. Juanita crying and pleading in the other room was unnerving. Slocum was waiting on Sims's answer.

"Let's go," Sims said to the pair, and started to leave.

"Sims, you got something to say, say it."

He cut his brown-eyed glare around to Slocum. "I's don't know you business up here. Maybe you's should find a new country."

"That a threat?"

Sims shrugged. "You got ears."

Anger fuming out of Slocum, he watched the big man turn his back to him and then follow the other two out. Slocum followed them to the doorway. They mounted and turned their horses into the dark night without a word.

Juanita's screams of grief rang in his ears as the three rode away. Had it really been an accident? Manuel's death?

Somehow, he felt that Sims had not expected to find anyone but Juanita at the stage stop. He didn't bring the corpse back because he was a good guy. The big man had a purpose in all this.

"They say anything else?" Collie Bill asked from behind Slocum as he stood out under the stars watching them ride away.

"No. He told me to leave."

"Sims?"

"Who else? What can I do?"

"Ride up and get Señora Peralta. Juanita wants her to help make the arrangements."

"I won't be back for several hours." How far it was to the ranch he had no idea, but it wasn't close by.

Collie Bill nodded. "I can hold things here."

"I need to ask her some directions."

Collie Bill agreed, and let him in the side room. On her knees beside the bed, Juanita was clutching her dead husband's hand and sobbing

"Juanita, I'm sorry, but I need some help on directions to find the señora's ranch."

She raised her wet face, nodded, and swallowed. "You follow the creek road. You can't miss the main headquarters."

"I'll be back with her as soon as I can."

Woodenly, she nodded and turned away as a new flood of tears filled her eyes. Collie Bill thanked Slocum and then knelt beside her to hug her shoulder. "He'll bring her back here," he told Juanita.

Slocum left under the stars. The snow had stopped, but fast-passing clouds still cut off the starlight now and then. He short-loped Heck a good ways on the road, which was paved with round creek stones. It was marshy in some places from the melted snow. His sheepskin coat protected him from the cold wind, and he wondered how far away the señora's place was.

Well past midnight by his calculation, he found the ranch headquarters and several dogs barked. He dismounted at the rack and studied the dark two-story house towering above him. His raps on the door were loud, and echoed beyond the tall double doors. He waited, shifting his weight from foot to foot.

"Who are you?" a voice husky with sleep demanded.

"My name is Slocum. There's been a death. I must talk to the señora."

"Go away. The señora's asleep this time of night. Come back in the morning."

He drew a deep breath. "Lady, either you open that door or I'm busting in."

"Who is out there, Anita?" It sounded like Perla.

"He calls himself Slo-cum. He says there has been a death."

"Open the door."

"Sí, señora." And the bolt latch shifted and the door creaked on its hinges, opening cautiously.

"Thank you," Slocum said, and went under the arch into the main room. In the dim light, he saw her like an angel in a shaft of light halfway down the stairs. Dressed in layers of white lace nightgown, she looked anxiously at him, waiting for him to speak.

Hat in hand, he spoke to her from below. "Manuel was killed today. Juanita, his wife, sent me to get you to come and help her."

"How did he die?" In the dim light, she looked her usual aloof self.

"They said he was thrown from his horse and broke his neck."

"Oh, poor Juanita. I will dress and be down. Anita, feed him. He always fed me well."

He nodded and replaced his hat. In a flurry of lace, she hurried up the wide staircase. Still the same woman he'd first met on the road. She'd never let her guard down, even in times of crisis.

"Señor. Señor." It was the older woman, Anita, trying to get his attention.

"Sorry," he said, realizing how engrossed in Perla he had been. He fell in behind the woman, going across the tile floor and under one of the keystone arches that ringed the open two-story center of the house, which surrounded a fountain. He could hear the soft sound of its splashing water.

"She will be ready shortly," said Anita.

"I know. She is never slow about such things."

"You know her well then."

"Has she always been so—reserved?"

Anita lighted the lamp on a table in the dark kitchen that smelled of food and cooking. Her dark brown eyes were like liquid pools of concern. "No, Señor. Once she laughed and would have taken your arm and dragged you in here laughing and teasing you about what she could fix for you."

"She must have been fun then."

"Oh, she was. This house danced with excitement and fun. Her laughter was like a silver bell and we all enjoyed our jobs. But the night he killed the *patrón* brought silence to this casa and the whole ranch."

"Who killed him?"

"The—the bandits." She busied herself wrapping some cooked meat into a tortilla.

"No, you said *he* came and shot her husband."

She looked away and would not face him.

"I am asking you because you know who shot him." He moved swiftly around the table and took hold of her shoulders, forcing her to look at him. "You know his name."

She drew back. "I can't tell you. I have sworn to never—"

"Tell me who it is. All I've heard is vagueness about these bandits. You know who did it. Tell me." He shook her.

"I can't. I swore on my life never to tell anyone. We could all be killed."

"Who was it?"

"Tell him, Anita."

He whirled, and Perla was standing in the doorway wearing her riding clothing. "This man has had a death wish since I first met him."

15

Slocum turned back to Anita and released his fierce hold on her arms. She dropped to her knees and, holding her hands clasped in prayer, she began to sob. "But Señor, they will come on us like wolves."

"Who shot the *patrón*?" Slocum insisted, looking back and forth at Anita and Perla for an answer.

"Mother of God—" Anita's voice cracked. "We have no one to protect us. The pistoleros are gone."

"Tell him," Perla said softly yet commandingly.

"The mulatto," spilled off Anita's trembling lips.

Then Anita fell sobbing on the tile floor. "They will kill us all," she cried.

He swung on his heel and faced Perla. "He's the one that raped you?"

Expressionless, she met his gaze. "You once said to shoot, not wait. I was foolish enough to think he would respect who I was."

"You told the law you didn't know them."

Her eyelids narrowed. "The law would not be here when they returned. What should I have told them?"

He nodded. "And they have returned, haven't they?"

"I never said—"

He shook his head, knowing the real answer. They had returned. Shuddering in fury, he turned to pound his fists on the table. "I asked you to let me—"

"Shall we ride to the stage stop? I am certain Juanita needs me."

He dropped his chin in defeat. "Let's go."

Outside in the cold, starry night, he led Heck with Perla down to the stables, and Diego was up with a lamp to meet them. In minutes, he had the gray stallion saddled. They went through the darkness without a word, the horses' hooves crunching the refrozen snow. An occasional snort of their mounts, the jingle of the bits in the horses' mouths, and the creak of saddle leather rode over the silence between them. The cold still night was illuminated by the ghostly reflection off the white ground cover. He rode not three feet from her and the proud stallion breathing clouds of vapor in the air. Yet she could have been three miles from him, for she neither turned aside nor did she speak as the hours rolled by.

"You can hide behind your silence as long as you want. But someday, it will fester like a boil and explode."

She turned and looked at him. Her eyes were shaded some by the flat-crowned hat that she wore atop a silk scarf to cover her head from the cold. "You don't understand. My people and I have to live under their threat. They can come anytime and extract whatever they want from us—we are helpless to resist them and nothing will change that."

"It could."

"You do not understand. Tomorrow or the next day you will be gone. We must remain here and answer to what you would do for us."

Grimly, he nodded in reply. He had no intention of leaving until the matter of the Boosters and Sims was settled. Somehow, he'd settle it. But there was no way he could convince her of anything—she held on to the ranch by a straw. They didn't rob her. They extracted her money and cattle by simply riding up and demanding it. They had her right where they wanted her—afraid and vulnerable.

"The law. They have never offered you any protection?"

"What law? A sheriff fifty miles away. How much law is that?"

He shook his head. It was long past his bedtime, and arguing was doing no good. If only she'd accept his help—no way that she would—they had her convinced and afraid, perhaps more for her people than even herself. It would be an uphill battle if he even started it, and he had no one but Collie Bill to help him. There were few other men he'd trust backing him like he would Collie Bill, but it wasn't *his* war either.

There had to be a way. He glanced over at her and saw her chin raised as she looked ahead. She had nothing to say. The horses' hooves crushing the frozen crust was the only sound in the cold night. They rode on.

What would it be like to have her in his arms? To hold that lithe body by the waist and raise her up to his face to kiss her mouth with its rose-petal lower lip. Damn, what a shame. She was such a block of ice and there was no heat to melt her down.

A peach tinge painted the eastern sky when they arrived at the stage stop. They dismounted heavily and Slocum hung on to the saddle horn until his sea legs were solid under him.

"I'll put up the horses," he said, and she nodded. He watched her bound onto the porch and then disappear inside. Gone again. She'd evaporated like smoke. He shook his head, unhitching the gray and leading the two horses off to the corrals and outbuildings.

Her gray tossed his bit in his teeth, arched his neck, and loudly nickered with authority to the others in the night. Slocum shook his head. Maybe riding a stud was her answer. The gray must be her show of defiance toward the outlaws. He'd take a gelding any day. Mares and studs were unreliable. At last, he had the gray in a box stall. Then Heck was grained and turned out.

"You going to live down here?" Collie Bill asked, coming out in the night looking for him.

"I'm through. How's Juanita?" He slung an arm over Collie Bill's shoulder. "She going to make it?"

"She's tough enough she'll make it. When the smoke clears, I'm going to offer to stay and help her. Then her and I can see how things work—I mean between us."

"I understand. You've been taken with her from the start, haven't you?"

Collie Bill nodded. "It might not work out, but I want to see."

"Good luck. I learned something else up at the Peralta Ranch. It wasn't some outlaws robbed and raided the ranch, it was Sims and the Booster bunch."

Collie Bill stopped dead in his tracks, and Slocum disengaged his arm. "I got her to admit it. They live in terror of them coming back. Her, her help, and a few Mexican ranch hands."

"What else?"

"Sims was one of them that raped her."

"One of them?"

"She wouldn't tell me more. I suspect the Booster brothers helped themselves as well."

After a check around to be certain they were alone, Collie Bill shook his head. "I think the reason Manuel was supposedly gone the other day—he didn't want to encounter them."

"Juanita, too?"

Collie Bill nodded. "It ain't what she's said, it's what she hasn't said. You recall the day you made them pay for lunch?"

"Yes."

"I saw something like deep fear in her eyes when they first arrived. Just a guess, but I still think there is something there."

"We better get in there before my knees buckle."

"Sorry, you've been up all night. I caught a little shut-eye. Go get some sleep. I'll start the grave."

"Hell, I'd not even thought about that."

"Don't worry, I won't have it all dug by the time you wake up."

Slocum smiled and they went inside the warm room together. He didn't see the women. He went straight to the shed on the side, slipped off his boots, undid his holster, hung it with his hat on a peg, and was in the bedroll. When his head hit the pillow, he was fast sleep.

Perla came under the arch toward him, dressed in the layered lace nightgown that glowed in the shaft of moonlight. Her long hair, unbraided, was tied back, and she paused at a distance from him beside the fountain's knee-high walls.

"You wanted my body?"

"Yes." There, he'd admitted it.

"You have lusted for my body?" She folded her arms and glared at him.

"You know that?"

A knock on the door made him turn.

"Ignore that. They can stay outside there. I am talking to you."

"I have been intrigued by you since we first met on the road."

"Why? You know I am little more than a *puta* for outlaws."

"That's not your will." The knocking grew louder and made him anxious to answer it with his gun or whatever.

"I do it. I sell my body for my life and the lives of my loyal workers."

"Perla, let me care for you—"

The door burst open and Sims rushed in. He laughed at seeing Slocum, as if Slocum posed no threat whatsoever, and swept her up in his arms. "Come on, little cunt. We got's business to do up in your feather bed."

Slocum's feet would not move, they were glued to the tile. He drew his gun, aimed it at the laughing bastard's back going up the staircase with her, and the hammer clicked on empty—

"Wake up. Wake up. You were screaming."

He blinked, looking into Perla's concerned brown eyes. She was on her knees beside the bed and when he searched her face, she dropped her chin. "I see you are all right now."

His hand caught her by the wrist before she could rise. "I was having a nightmare. Do you have nightmares?"

She didn't struggle, but settled down again beside him. "Yes, I have them often."

He nodded. "I shared one of yours last night."

With a nod, she agreed. Then she wet her lips. "I have not been fair to you. But there is no way for me to accept your gallantry. Juanita is asleep. We will have Manuel's funeral late today."

"I need to—"

She pushed him back down. "Sleep some more. Others are helping."

"I can't—"

"Yes, you can. The dream is over. Get some rest." She rose, gathering her divided skirt. "Later, we will have a large meal. Do you have a Bible?"

"Yes."

"The nearest priest is miles away. He can say Mass later. Will you read and pray for Manuel?"

"I'm not Catholic."

"Neither was Jesus." She rose, then pulled down the hem of her vest and the armor was in place. "Sleep."

Wistfully, he watched her swish out of the shed, closed his sore eyes, and fell back asleep.

The dull sun blazed in the western sky. Most of the clouds had gone away, but a bitter cold north wind swept down off the Rockies. With his back to the wind, he read from the pages of Psalms. By his estimation, Manuel was a man of those verses.

"Yea, though I walk through the valley of death . . ." Slocum read slowly and loud enough so all could hear him. In the end, when he said amen, they echoed him.

Juanita stood between Collie Bill and Perla. Both women were under black shawls, and they crossed themselves when he finished. Many of the quiet people who had helped dig the grave came by and shook Collie Bill's hand with a softly spoken *"Gracias."*

Three of the younger men were refilling the grave. They waved Slocum and Bill away. "We can do this."

"Come inside when you finish," Juanita said to them, and Collie Bill led her away. "We have much food," she said over her shoulder.

Slocum turned, and was startled when he found Perla standing there waiting. She put her gloved hand in the crook of his arm, and he led her back to the stage stop at the foot of the small hill.

"You did very well back there." Her voice was soft, like a whisper on the wind. "You are a man of many talents. Why do you have no roots?"

"The war. Other things that I never planned on happening."

"Life can become hell."

"But even the devil can be stopped."

"I have prayed for that, too. Now Manuel is dead. Do you think he really died from his horse throwing him?"

"I have no way to know."

"I wonder when I will wake up and this nightmare will be over."

"There are ways, Perla. There are ways to do that."

She shook her head and released his arm at the front door. "I cannot chance their lives. Thanks again. You are a big man, Slocum. The more I know you, the more I see that. But there are too many of them."

"I have to go to Española and look for a stage robber. When I return, may I call on you?"

She blinked her eyes. "You are a lawman, too?"

He checked around in the twilight and satisfied they were alone, spoke softly. "I work for the express company they robbed."

With a sharp nod, she swallowed hard. "I must go in and help the other women serve the food—" She swung her skirt around, then paused with her back to him. "I am sorry, but I think for you to visit me would only provoke them."

"Yes, ma'am."

She went inside. He stood for a moment in the cold wind. He'd heard the warning of Sims for him to get out. It made more sense to him now than it had at the time. He needed One-Eye turned over to the authorities and then he'd get back up to Perla's ranch. Under the circumstances, it might be hard for Collie Bill to pull away from Juanita. He wasn't sure about Bledstone—but he'd soon figure him out on the way to Española.

The man was due to arrive there anytime.

16

Bledstone arrived the next morning on the stage. He carried his felt hat in his hand and looked like he was hurting as he got out of the coach. His head was bandaged and both eyes were black.

"What got hold of you?" Collie Bill asked.

Bledstone shook his head wearily. "Sumbitches tried to kill me."

"Didn't I warn you?"

"Yeah, but they was in her room waiting on me. Had her tied and gagged on the bed. I got a shot off. I hit one of them. Then they knocked me out and used their boots on me. I reckon they were spooked by that shot of mine and worried about the guy I shot, so they fled."

"She know who they were?"

"If she did, she wouldn't say. You know whores' lives are cheap."

"You talk to Thorpe?" Slocum asked.

"Oh, yeah, before I left." Bledstone lowered his voice. "One-Eye robbed another stage. Thorpe heard that the boy he calls Kid is living with a Mexican woman in Española. He thinks he's our best lead to Davis."

Slocum looked around to make sure the driver and the two other passengers were inside the building. Then he spoke. "What's her name?"

111

"Tonyah Vasquez."

Slocum looked at Collie Bill. He shook his head. "Must be one I missed."

"She lives on the road east," said Bledstone.

"We can find her," Slocum said. "Collie has to stay here. The woman's husband was killed in a wreck and he's helping her."

"Damnit, I thought—" Bledstone looked pissed at the news.

"We ain't going after Jesse James. They're three two-bit stage robbers."

"Yeah, but what if?"

"What if what? Get some food inside. You and me're taking the stage down there and getting them," Slocum said, out of patience. He wanted to settle with Sims, and staying at the Flores place another day would only prolong the whole business.

"All right. All right. You never were beat to a pulp like I was."

"Goes with the territory. Is Thorpe coming down?"

"Yeah, he said he'd be down there in three days and help us." Slocum shook his head. "They'll be in the jail by then."

"He wanted in on arresting them."

"You better go eat." Slocum folded his arms over his chest. He'd need his saddlebags, .44/40 Winchester, and bedroll.

Collie Bill looked concerned. "I could go."

"No, she needs you here. Don't take on Sims if you can avoid it. I'll be back and handle him."

"What do you expect to happen down there?"

"We'll find the Kid and he'll tell us where the others are at."

"What if he won't?"

"There's ways to get trash like that to talk."

Collie Bill nodded, looking put out. "I know you counted on me."

"I'll be fine." Slocum looked up and Perla was on the porch. With concern written on her face, she beckoned to him.

"I'll go see what I can do to help," Collie Bill said to excuse himself.

"Sure," Slocum said, and walked over to where Perla stood.

"Yes?"

"This is the express man? What happened to him?"

Slocum looked up at her on the porch. "That's him all right. He looks pretty, doesn't he?"

"Who did that?" She frowned. Small lines appeared in her smooth forehead.

"I think one of your neighbors, Cal Booster."

"These men won't stop at anything." She folded her arms and looked away.

"Right now we have some stage robbers to go see about in Española."

"Who?"

"That one-eyed man we met on the road and his gang."

She nodded. "Collie is staying with Juanita? I hope that he is going to—she needs him."

"Yes." He looked hard at her, but she never returned his gaze. "I have to get my things. Anything else?"

"No." She moved to go inside, and he about bumped into her when she stopped reaching for the door handle and turned around.

He was too close. They were inches apart and she drew in her breath. For a moment, she looked ready to faint. Then, to escape his eyes, she put her forehead on his chest and squeezed his arms. "God be with you, Slocum. I will burn a candle for your safety."

"Thank you."

"I know you are not a Catholic."

"Any faith is good. You have a strong one."

With that, she opened the door and hurried for the kitchen, leaving him on his own.

"I'll be taking the stage to Española," he said to the driver, who was cradling a cup of coffee.

"Fine, get your things. We'll be heading out of here in five minutes."

"Collie, get my saddlebags and Winchester. I'll tie up the bedroll."

"Gotcha." Collie Bill left on the run.

In the end, he added his saddle to the boot in back in case

they needed to rent horses. He shook Collie Bill's hand, hugged Juanita, and nodded to Perla.

"I'll be back in five days."

"Be careful," Juanita said. "Thank you for all you have done for me."

He waved and slipped into the coach beside the grumbling Bledstone. He saw Perla standing there even after the other two went inside. Leaving her there hurt him, but she wasn't ready for help. When she was, she could invite him to her ranch. He'd left that door open.

"That Mexican bitch is sweet on you," Bledstone said.

"You mean Señora Peralta?"

"Yeah, the old snow queen. She's a widow, too?"

Slocum shed his remarks like a duck does water. He settled his back against the seat. They should have taken the backward-facing seat; that was the better one to ride. "Yes and she's hardly stuck on me."

"Fooled me. That's Whistler." Bledstone motioned to the bald-headed drummer. "And the other one is Phillips." He was younger and dressed in miner's clothing and high-top lace-up boots.

"Nice to meetcha," Slocum said, removing his hat and leaning back to sleep in the rocking coach, complete with the sound of harnesses and horses' hooves and the ring of the iron rims rocking him to slumber.

Slocum woke up at the various stops. The other three were playing five-card poker for nickels and Bledstone was losing. He couldn't even draw a high card when the others had nothing.

By the time they reached Española the next day, Slocum was worn out, his belly hurt from bad food, and he was tired of Bledstone's whining about losing nickels, his sore head and body, and how tired he was. They went to the Alhambra Hotel and got separate rooms. Slocum went out and found a bath, a shave, and a haircut. Some Oriental cleaned his clothes while he bathed, and the barber thought the Vasquez woman lived on the Truchas Road somewhere up near Chamayo.

Slocum paid him and went to the cantina across the street. For forty cents, he bought two full fingers of whiskey and the word that Tonyah Vasquez lived on the right across the second dry wash past the church on the Chamayo/Truchas Road. The whiskey cleared some of the staleness from his mouth. He left the cantina and walked to the livery. Most of the snow was gone at this low altitude. It was late afternoon, and he rented a horse and buggy for a day.

"I am going to see my aunt in Chamayo. I will be back in the morning," he told the livery man.

"What is her name?"

"You know people up there?"

"Oh, yes," the man said and beamed. "I know many people up there."

"What is your name?"

"Victor Obregon."

"I will tell my aunt I have met you. Maybe she will know you." He clicked to the horse and swung him into the traffic.

"Wait! Wait!" the man shouted. "What is her name?"

Slocum waved to him and made the horse trot away. Her name was Tonyah Vasquez and the bartender in Franco's Cantina said there were prettier whores upstairs than her. But the stable man didn't need to know his business either.

He couldn't risk anyone knowing his business—at least no more than necessary to find out information. If he could bring in the Kid that evening, maybe they could ride out and take One-Eye and the old man Nelson before they were spooked off. Then they could wire Thorpe and he could come take them.

Past sundown, he went by the small dark church and crossed two dry washes that had spread sand across the hard-packed road. The second one had some tailwater from an irrigation ditch overflow coming down it. He reined the horse to the side of the road. The jacal sat under some gnarled bare cottonwoods. With the horse tied to a fence post, Slocum checked his Colt and crept up on the place.

Easing his way to the dimly lit window, he could see through the distorted glass a naked chunky girl lying on her back with a hatchet-assed boy pounding her. Slocum about laughed as he went around to the front door and listened to their efforts and hard breathing. Quietly, he raised the latch with the string they'd so generously left out for him, and the door creaked on the hinges as it swung open.

Bug-eyed, the Kid looked back in half stride on top of her. "What—"

She screamed as the Kid, with his waving pole, scrambled off her onto his knees. By then Slocum had him by the hair of his head and held him up off his butt. The chunky girl had crawfished to the head of the bed and looked in wide-eyed fear at the gun Slocum held on them. Her short drawn-up legs resembled stuffed sausages, and her wide belly was like bread dough around her deep navel, with a large patch of curly black pubic hair below that.

"I ain't asking you twice," said Slocum. "Where's One-Eye Davis?"

The Kid shook his head. Slocum drove the pistol muzzle into his privates and cocked the hammer back. "You won't ever screw anyone ever again after I pull this trigger."

"He's in—in Bernallio."

"Where?" He jabbed the gun hard into the Kid's scrotum.

"Tell him. Dear Jesus, tell him!" the girl screamed.

"At his mother's house. It is down by the river."

"What's her name?"

"Felicia—Gawd, man, I'm telling you, please don't shoot me."

"What's her name?"

"Felicia Moore. Her new husband is Phillip Moore. They live on a farm on the Rio Grande. I swear to God that is where he is at."

Slocum jerked on his hair. "When is he coming back here?"

"In a week or so."

"No, when?"

"Next week there is a stage coming . . ."

"What stage?"

The Kid's erection had dissolved and he no longer offered any resistance. Slocum shoved him down on his back across the bed. "Now, where's Nelson?"

"In Española. He lives with some old woman."

"What's her name?"

"Hell, I don't know—"

"Valerie—" the large-eyed naked girl said, with her back pressed hard to the wall to get as far away from Slocum as she could.

"Valerie what?"

"Valerie Myrez."

"Good girl."

She looked a little relieved at that and drew in a deep breath. "What else do you need?"

"I'm going to tie you two up while I go get my partner. I won't be gone long, but if you try to escape while I'm gone, when I catch you I'll cut his pecker off square with his belly."

They both nodded gravely.

"Get over in this chair," he ordered the boy.

He obeyed, and Slocum soon had his hands secured behind his back and him bound to the seat. Then he ripped a strip off the old sheet and made a gag and a blindfold for him. Then he motioned for her to get on her belly.

"You won't hurt me, will you?"

He blinked at her. What she meant was some kind of sadistic sex. "No, but if you two escape while I am gone, you know what I'll do."

"Oh, we won't, I promise. I swear to the Virgin Mary."

He couldn't risk One-Eye learning his two henchmen were in jail and then hitting the high road. They needed Nelson, too. But he couldn't deliver them to the law—not yet. Bledstone wouldn't be happy over this all-nighter. With her facedown on the bed, he looked at her plump ass as he tied her ankles. Maybe Bledstone could take that out on her.

He gagged and blindfolded her. No need in taking any chances. Then he leaned down by her ear. "You two better be here when I get back."

She nodded her head vigorously and mumbled from behind the gag that they would be there. He put a few logs in the fireplace, blew out the candles, and hurried for the buggy. The trip to get his man would take two hours, if he was lucky.

The drive to town was effortless, and he was soon pounding

on Bledstone's hotel room door. "Get up. We've got business to take care of."

"That you, Slocum?"

Slocum looked at the tin tile ceiling for help in the dimly lighted hallway. "Who in the hell do you think is out here?"

His sleep-husky voice replied, "I didn't know." He cracked the door. "What now?"

"Get dressed. I've got the Kid and his girlfriend tied up at her place and we've got to get back there."

Standing in the dim light of the room, scratching his privates, Bledstone made a face at him. "Girlfriend?"

"We can't have anyone running to One-Eye and warning him. Her included. And One-Eye don't need to hear we've captured his henchmen and decide to take a powder before we can arrest him."

Bledstone began pulling on his pants. "What's she look like?"

"Kinda plump. She's young and scared to death. I threatened to blow his balls off if he didn't tell me where One-Eye was. Him and her were naked on the bed when I caught them. He went to talking."

"I bet he did. Shit, I'd'a told you anything with a gun pointed at mine." He put up his suspenders. "We keeping them as prisoners for very long?"

"We're wiring Thorpe to get down here. Then he can decide what to do with them."

"Sure, sure, he wanted to be in on it."

"I want this wrapped up in a few days. I've got other things to do."

"Sure." Bledstone took down his suspenders to put on his shirt with his hair hanging in his face. Then he gave it a toss back that was only partially successful in clearing his vision.

Damn, Slocum missed Collie Bill already. Bledstone was not only dull-witted, he was slow.

Slocum sent a wire to Thorpe. Then, sharing the narrow seat with Bledstone's big butt, he trotted the buggy horse out on the road, which was shaded from the starlight by the towering bare cottonwoods. Their breath came in clouds in the cold night air. He was anxious to see if his prisoners were still there.

He reined up and they climbed down. "I'm unhitching the horse. Get your gun out and be ready. Go see about them."

"Sure." Bledstone went for the jacal with his gun in hand. There was no telling about him. Slocum unhitched the horse and put it in the pole corral with the Kid's horse. Coming back, he could see by looking in the small window that his man had the naked Tonyah, still tied, sitting up on the edge of the bed, and he was building up the fire in the small fireplace. Good. That meant the Kid was there, too.

Bledstone turned from his task when Slocum came inside. "Say, she ain't half bad-looking."

"I said she was all right."

"You mind if me and her do some business?"

Slocum shrugged. "I'm going to bed somewhere. You guard them." He looked into the dark side room with the low ceiling and saw the cot. "I'll be right in there if you need me."

The Kid's head hung down, he was half-asleep. No way Slocum wanted him to get some good sleep—his mind might go to figuring out a way for him to run off. He went over and jerked him upright. "You thinking about escaping?"

Still blindfolded and gagged, the Kid shook his head.

"Good, stay awake then." Slocum left Bledstone seated on the bed beside Tonyah, fondling her small breasts and talking to her. In the room, Slocum could hear her giggling about something. Then he lay down on the cot and pulled the sweat-stinking cotton blanket over himself. He awoke once, and could hear them breathing like runaway horses and grunting like pigs. He went back to sleep.

It was before dawn when he awoke. The fire was about out and he could see four bare half-moons sticking up on the bed. The Kid was slumped in the chair and Bledstone, with his arm slung over Tonyah, was snoring away. Fine guard he made. On his knees, Slocum stoked the fireplace coals, and then he set in some more split-aspen blocks on the red-hot ashes. The heat reflected off the coals felt good. Soon, flames were licking up and he rose.

One or the other of the two had pulled a blanket over them and then snuggled closer. Maybe she'd done it, because Bledstone had never missed a rasping snore.

Slocum slipped outside and emptied his bladder in a long stream. Everything was frosted under the starlight; the temperature must have really dropped overnight. Finished, he shook it and put it away. He had no intention of using his dick on Tonyah in there. He wiped his mouth on his calloused hand. In a week, he needed to be at May's cabin—he wanted to know all he could about the Booster operation before he took it on, and besides that, she sure wasn't half bad in bed either. A place where he'd probably never get to taste the sweetness of Perla Peralta.

He'd go back in, wake up Bledstone, hitch the horse, and go find Nelson. When they had Nelson and the Kid, he could set out for One-Eye. Thorpe would arrive shortly. Though Slocum didn't know the man, he'd known enough express agents. They didn't value road agents as worth much, and sure didn't bring many back to the law. In this case, Thorpe could do all that his way. Just so Slocum got the reward to split with Collie Bill.

Would Collie Bill stay hitched at Juanita's place? No telling. Maybe he'd learned enough lessons in life to settle down. At times, Slocum wished he could find an attractive woman like Juanita and spend the rest of his life growing old with her. But that would never work.

He opened the door, and in the red orange light could see Bledstone on his side, humping it to her from behind on top of the bed. He must have been starved for it.

"I'm going to find Nelson. I'll be back."

"Yeah," Bledstone said with his hair in his face. Half-raised up behind her, he looked up at Slocum, but never took his dick out of her. In fact, he steadied her hip and shoved it in her deeper. "I'll watch 'em."

"Do that." And fuck her—'cause he knew Bledstone would anyway. "I'll be back sometime with Thorpe."

"Yeah," Bledstone said as he slapped her on the butt to get

her up on her hands and knees. He never turned back, too busy with one hand on her bare shoulder to steady her and the other inserting his erection in her from behind. Down on her elbows underneath him, she moaned in a sleepy voice. Slocum left them.

17

"Valerie Myrez?" Slocum asked the sleepy bartender as he looked over the brown whiskey in his glass at the large nude painting over the back bar. The woman was plump. Not as plump as Tonyah, but she had a swell to her belly and a dark patch of pubic hair. Tonyah had a blanket of that stuff that covered her entire V. But where Tonyah's midsection looked like gobs of dough, this one was sleek. Her breasts were pear-shaped with pink caps—Tonyah's looked like pouches with swollen black nipples that pointed at you.

The bartender curled his lip. "There are much better *putas* than Myrez."

"I'm not looking for ass. She knows something I need to know."

He nodded. "Go to the river and turn right at the new bridge. She lives in the third jacal. In her front yard, she has a statue of a man carved from a log. You can't miss it."

Slocum downed the whiskey and slapped two quarters on the counter. One for the drink, one for the barkeep.

Picking them up, the man nodded in approval. "*Gracias.* But I hope you find something better than her to fuck."

They both laughed.

A short while later, Slocum drove the buggy up to the jacal the bartender told him about, climbed down, and watched a

122

red-tailed rooster begin to crow on top of the pole corral. With the lead rope, he tied the horse to the old *carreta* and headed for the house.

He could hear two people inside loudly arguing in Spanish. The words he could make out were, "He's the law. Who told him? He's the damn law!"

Six-gun in hand, he charged the front door. Using a well-planted boot where he thought the latch was, he smashed it. His force tore the hinges out of the frame, broke any latch, and flattened the door in a cloud of dust on the floor.

Her shrill scream cut the room's darkness, but he could see the back door was wide open. His man was already gone. He rushed through the jacal, out the back way, and saw where Nelson'd hit the head-high willows. In fact, he could see the tops of the leafless brown willows moving as Nelson made his attempt to escape. Slocum took the rail fence by laying his hand on it and flipping himself over it.

The branches tore at him as he ran through the dense growth, but ahead he could hear Nelson coughing. He wouldn't run far if he was that bad off. Slocum burst out into a small alfalfa patch and spotted him bent over trying to get his breath.

"Come with me. We're going to see your buddy the Kid."

The man blinked his eyes at Slocum. "You got him, too?"

"All we need now is One-Eye. Where's he at?" It was a test to see if Nelson's answer matched Tonyah's and the Kid's story.

"How should I know?"

Slocum spun him around. "Listen, if I get my gun out, I'll blow your ear off."

"How should I know where he is?"

"You ain't listening."

"All right. All right." Nelson held his hands up in surrender. "He's down there at his mother's house."

"What's her name?"

"She lives with this guy in Bernallio. Moore. She just married him."

"Good, we ain't lying to each other."

"What're you doing with me?"

"Holding you for the express company agent."

Nelson's shoulders dropped. "Why didn't you shoot me back there and get it over with?"

"I ain't shooting no one that don't resist arrest with deadly force."

"He will."

"That's between you and him. How do you know that he will?"

"I was running with some guys down by El Paso one time. We held up a stage, got a little money, and went to this whore-house across the border. We was all busy fucking them girls. Those express men must have followed our footprints. Three of them broke in there. The whore I was with hid me under her bed. But them bastards made them other three boys get on their hands and knees, faces on the floor right there beside the bed I was under. Then they shot each one of them in the back of the head and took all the money those gals had.

"I still can't hear good. I've got some money stashed, I can pay you."

"Give it to her. I've already cut my deal with them."

"I sure as hell won't need it wherever I'm going, will I?" He climbed through the fence.

Valerie came running holding a towel to her mouth. She was gray-headed and tired-looking, her beauty long faded. Her breasts hung low and her belly sagged. "What will happen to him?"

"That's up to the law."

"He's lying," said Nelson. "He ain't the law, he's the fucking express company."

Her eyes widened. "Please, oh, please, I beg of you don't kill him." She fell to her knees and held her hands flat together in prayer. "I beg of you in the name of God . . ."

"Tell her where the money is hidden." Slocum gave Nelson a nudge.

Her eyes flickered in disbelief from one to the other of them. "What money?"

"It's in a can, buried under the horse manger." Nelson nodded toward the corral.

"How much?" She was regaining her feet and wiping her

tears on the towel. Then she rushed over and hugged him. "Oh, I will miss you so much. Come back to me."

Nelson was looking over the top of her head, trying not to encourage her. "That ain't going to happen. Let's go, mister."

They were on the Chamayo road headed east when Slocum asked him, "Was there much money there?"

"Enough she will live like a rich old woman."

Slocum nodded. He reined the horse into the yard and stopped Nelson before he climbed down. "Don't try anything. We'll kill you in a second."

Nelson shrugged. "What's the difference? Now or later?"

"I ain't the executioner. That's up to the agent, but you cross me or try anything foolish, you're dead."

Nelson nodded.

Slocum knocked, then opened the door. Tonyah bolted up in bed still undressed, and the bleary-eyed Bledstone's hairy chest was exposed right beside her.

"Oh, you're back. That Nelson?" Bledstone blinked his eyes in disbelief.

"That's him. I'm riding south to get One-Eye. Better have her get dressed and go after some food. You'll be here awhile"

The downcast Kid was still naked, but handcuffed to a chair and seated at the table. Bledstone was up and pulling on his pants. He produced a second set of handcuffs and put one on Nelson's wrist. Then he led him over to the table and put the other cuff on the chair the Kid was cuffed to. He stuck a chair under Nelson and nodded in approval at his arrangement. "They'll be here until Thorpe comes."

"Good. I'll leave him word at the hotel where you are at if I am not back."

"Good, I wondered how I'd do that. You realize we have a thousand dollars sitting here?"

"Three hundred and thirty-three apiece."

"Huh?"

"Collie Bill gets his share."

"He ain't even here."

"No, but he's cut in on the deal. Now get her ass dressed and send her after some food."

"You staying for it?" he asked, hustling Tonyah's fat butt out of the bed. Without a word, she began to wiggle into her skirt and then pulled the blouse on over her head

"No," Slocum said. "I'm going after One-Eye. Nelson said he was at his mother's place, too."

"You may need backup."

"Tonyah," Slocum said, ignoring him and staring hard at her. "You tell a soul what's happening here, I'll know." He made a slicing motion with his hand across his throat. "But you be good and keep your mouth shut, you'll have money in your hand when we leave. Savvy?"

With both hands, she swept her coarse short hair back from her face. "*Sí,* I savvy *muy bien.*"

"That's good. Bledstone, don't forget her pussy ain't the only reason you're here. It may take Thorpe two days to get down here."

"What about you?"

"I'm going to go get One-Eye. I'll bring him back or his head. We'll get that reward."

"Cuting it three ways don't—"

"Quit bitching. I've done all the damn work up till now. We split three ways."

"All right." Bledstone was digging in his pants pocket for some money for Tonyah. "Get some meat. Fresh meat and a bottle of whiskey."

"I need flour and lard to make tortillas. I need frijoles," she went on, spelling out her needs.

Satisfied things were all right, Slocum went out, unhitched the horse, and drove back to Española. It was near four o'clock when he reached the livery. The next southbound stage was due in at eight that evening. He used his express pass to secure a ticket to Santa Fe. Fom there, he might ride a horse. At the hotel, he had them store Bledstone's things, and left a sealed envelope for Thorpe at the desk with a note on how to find Bledstone and the prisoners. Then he settled his and Bledstone's bills. That completed, he crossed to the telegraph office and wired Thorpe.

HAVE TWO OF THEM SEE MY LETTER AT
ALHAMBRA HOTEL DESK BLEDSTONE

"He'll sure as hell know that came from here, won't he?"
he asked the key operator.

"Sure, unless you want it sent from somewhere else."

Slocum shook his head. "That's good enough. How much
do I owe you?"

"A dollar would do."

After he settled with the man, he went to find supper. In a
Mexican café, he ordered some fire-browned beef, frijoles,
and a stack of fresh-made flour tortillas to wrap them in. The
waitress was a saucy talker, and swung her hips around serving the customers, but she made a nice diversion while his
food was being prepared.

The stage to Santa Fe was crowded with himself and three
other passengers. It was late evening the next day when it
reached the Santa Fe plaza. Stiff and sore from the ride, he
checked his saddle, bedroll, and rifle with the stage line agent,
and went off to look over the various joints around the square.
A cold north wind swept the streets. He kept back in the shadows when he entered the first saloon. The smoky interior held
a thick yellow haze that dimmed even the candle lamps overhead so they could hardly penetrate it. Unless a man was face-
to-face with somebody, he wouldn't know his own brother.

There were lots of fine *putas* laughing and showing off their
legs dancing to some trumpet player's sharp music. Castanets
clacked, and then some soprano voice began to sing in Spanish. The night was about to begin. Faro wheels spun and many
poker players, from dressed-up dandies to bathless freighters,
tossed money and coins on the tables as the cards were dealt.
Then he saw her. She wore a black dress buttoned to the top of
her throat and was wrapped in a black cape. Seated at the head
of the table, she shuffled a new deck and talked with the ease
of a man to the other gamblers.

She looked up once in his direction, but if she saw him, not a
muscle flinched in her cold face. He moved to the bar, ordered

a beer, and was resting his elbows on the bar when he saw her approaching in the mirror hanging over the back bar. Hugging the cape tight, she moved in beside him and spoke to the bartender.

"Tell that little bitch waiting on my table to keep those drinks coming."

The bartender nodded.

The she turned to him. "You in town for long?"

He shook his head.

"I get off at nine."

"I'll be here then."

"Fine, we can do the town after that." She shrugged her narrow shoulders, pulled the cape tight around herself, and left him in a swish of stiff material.

He finished his beer and paid the barkeep a dime, then slipped out of the place. He found a street vendor on the plaza squatted beside a small stove. Her head was wrapped in a scarf, and she looked up when he stopped beside her.

"You are hungry?" she asked. "My food is fresh every day. Each day my children eat what I have not sold."

"What do you have?"

"Beef, frijoles, and I can make a tortilla."

"Do that." He squatted across from her and rubbed his hands in the heat from her small stove.

"You have no woman to cook for you?" she asked as the strips of marinated meat sizzled with the cut-up pepper and onions.

He shook his head.

"You should find a young woman and raise some children of your own. A woman who can cook you good food and fill your bed on a cold night like this one. I bet I could find you one."

"No, I can't have a wife now." He wanted to tell her *never,* but that sounded too harsh for a nice woman so worried about him.

"Ah, you look for fancy one, huh?" Her hands were patting out a large flour tortilla, swirling it in a circular motion as she flattened it. Then she moved the brown meat and vegetables aside and put the white disk on the grill.

"I have no place for one."

"It will be very cold tonight. Do you have someone to sleep with tonight?"

"Yes, I do."

She nodded and turned the tortilla over, using her fingertips to pick it up and slap it back down. "Such a big man as you must have no trouble finding such company."

The white sheet was soon in her palm, and she was laying the meat and vegetables on it. Then deftly, she wrapped it up.

"How much do I owe you?" he asked.

"Ten cents."

He paid her two silver dollars. "How many children are yours to feed tonight?"

"Five." She looked in disbelief at the money in her palm.

"So many?"

"One is my sister's who was killed six months ago." She crossed herself. "Two are my cousin Martinia's children. I have them because where she works, she can't keep them."

He nodded. She probably worked in a whorehouse. "You have a man?"

She shook her head. "He ran off with a young girl for Mexico, I think."

After this first bite, he said, "He was a poor judge of women to leave such a good cook."

She rose and smiled at him. "What is your name?"

"Slocum."

"That is all?"

He nodded and took another bite. "What is yours?"

"Dolores Madereya."

"Good to meet you, Dolores. Hug those children for me."

"I will." Her face beamed. "They will pray for you at Mass."

"You think I need their prayers?"

"Sí. I have seen some bad things that are ahead for you. There is danger in the way."

"Do you see these men's faces so I would know them?"

"One never turns his head for me to see him."

"Could he have a patch on the one eye you don't see?"

She nodded. "Maybe."

"There are others?"

"*Sí.*"

"*Gracias.*" He left her and went to another saloon. *Brujas* like Dolores were to be listened to and he needed to heed her warning. Her concern showed. Would One-Eye be the worst? Or the Boosters and Sims? Time was ticking away. His line shack reunion with Miss Booster wasn't far off.

He downed the beer he'd ordered at the bar wondering what Mary had on her mind. It would soon be time to swing back by there for her. Damn, that woman's words earlier in the plaza had set him on edge—he needed to be careful.

18

Mary had her head held high, wearing a shawl over it. She swept outside in the darkness, looking around for him. Spotting him leaning against the building at the corner, she headed for him, her heels clicking on the stone walk.

He gave her the crook of his arm and she pointed eastward. Music spilled from behind the closed doors of the place. She paused, used her gloved hand to steady his face, and standing on her toes, kissed him on the mouth. His arms hugged her narrow form tight to him and he kissed her harder.

When their faces separated, a slow smile crossed the thin line of her mouth. "I should keep you in a cage, so I could come home each day and get in with you."

"We going inside?" He motioned to the door, not interested in being her kept pet.

"Yes, I want to dance with you." She ran her gloved palms over his leather coat.

"Fine." He reached past her and undid the knob. It was cold standing out there. Even kissing, it was cold. Inside, they danced to waltzes and polkas. The crowded place bubbled with couples. Some were good dancers, others shuffled, but there was no serious line drawn between them. Most of the people in the room were Hispanics, but they were polite, and teased him some once they decided he was not hostile.

A well-dressed man with gray temples came over when they were seated in a booth and introduced himself as Paul. Mary sat on Slocum's lap as if to cling closer to him, like she wanted to be wrapped inside of him.

"We have never met," Paul said, shaking his hand. "You here on business, if I may ask?"

"Only to see her, and then I must go."

"You know things in New Mexico are not well. We have many bandits and the law sits on its hands. I could use a man like you in my business."

"Your business?"

"Yes, I have a large family ranch. There are people who do not respect the fact my family has owned this land for a century and a half.

"They drive their cattle on our range and won't move them. Haul them to court, such a thing can take years, with delays and other things, before a judge will finally say—they don't belong there."

"I have many things I must do," said Slocum. "Sorry, I cannot help you."

"So am I sorry, too, for I see in you the man I need for this job."

Paul excused himself, and as Slocum watched the man leave, Mary took hold of Slocum's face and made him kiss her on the mouth. Slocum had forgotten how small her mouth was. His tongue filled it. Pressed hard to her, he felt the fire in her rising. His hand moved to feel her small breasts underneath the dress's lacy material.

She winked at him and pushed her chest at his hand. Then the band began playing a waltz. "I want to dance more. Soon you will leave me."

"Let us dance." They were soon on the smooth floor dancing across the corn meal that smoothed the less polished boards underfoot.

"That man Paul, he might pay you well for such a job." They swirled through the others.

"Would you come and be my wife while I worked for him?"

She frowned. "I'd never make a good wife for very long."

"I'd need a good wife to go with me out there."

"I would bet you can't even see a mountain from out there."

"Who needs mountains?"

She wrinkled her nose. "And the heat waves would make you think you were drunk every day. We better go to my place."

"Why?"

"Because I don't want to cry in public."

"Cry in public?"

"Yes." She pushed on his chest to make him leave the dance floor. "You asked me to be your wife—" She sniffed. "And like a damn fool I turned you down."

"It was only for—"

"Only for—" She blew her nose and tears sparkled in her lashes. "Hurry, please," she said as he put on his coat.

"I am hurrying."

Outside in the frigid night, she hugged him tight. "I know. I know. You could never stay on that ranch forever. Those Kansas deputies would show up looking for you. But—oh, Slocum—I would love to have you for as long as it would last."

"Tomorrow I need to go down to Bernallio and find a man."

"What did he do?"

"Robbed several stages."

"Then what?"

"There is a gang of outlaws exploiting ranchers up north."

Under his arm, she snuggled against him as they went down the stone sidewalk. "I hate it. I hate it."

"Won't do any good."

"Those stairs," she said, "go to my room." And she guided him to the base of the stairs.

He searched the dark night, and then nodded for her to go up first. On her heels, he went upstairs. At the top, she indicated the neat stack of wood beside the door and he took an armful inside.

She swept the hat off his head and let him go to the hearth. The fire was dead, and on his knees, he began making kindling with his knife, and soon struck a match to it. The pine shavings burst into flames, and he put the split wood over it. Soon, they would have heat.

In a few moments, she returned with blankets and a down comforter she spread on the floor before the emerging fire. "It will be warmer here than in the bed."

She took his coat and replaced it with a blanket over his shoulder. "There. I need you every night to make my fires. Mine never start that fast."

He unbuckled his gun, wrapped it up, and set it close by. The fire's growing flames were beginning to issue some heat and light the room up, casting his and her shadows on the wall.

She returned with a bottle of red wine, and on her knees before him she offered him some. He took a deep drink of the sweet grape, and then wiped his mouth on the back of his hand. She took the bottle and did the same. Then she bent over and kissed him.

"This will be a night I want to remember as I think how I could have had so many more such private fandangos with you."

He reached out and began to undo the tiny buttons one at a time on the front of her dress. It was really a blouselike top, and he knew that down by her waist it would be open. He went button by button in the fiery light to expose the snowy skin of her throat and chest. Then, when he reached the last button, he spread the blouse open more and gently cupped her small breasts.

She swooned, and put her hands on his shoulders, pressing the nipples against his palms. He bent over and kissed the right nipple, then the left, and she clutched him to it.

"Don't quit."

He wouldn't quit. She had no worries. It tasted like candy to him, and he was starved for more. While he sipped on her buds, she worked to shed her skirt and not interfere with what he was doing. At last, she pushed him back, and rose to get the skirt untangled from her legs and toss it in a chair.

He sat back and admired her willowy figure in the orange glow. Her legs were long, and would have taken any man's breath away. Her butt was small and her hips narrow—he could span her waist with both hands thumb to thumb—but the sight of her slender figure in the buff was enough to give him a hard-on when she dropped back on her knees before him.

She snatched up the wine bottle and offered him more. He took a swig, and then she did the same.

"I need that for courage to be here with you like this."

"Are you cold?"

"No, but I never undressed like this for anyone. Not even when I was married. He never ever saw me undressed."

"How did you make love?"

"Under the covers. I raised my nightgown up a short ways."

Slocum reached out and hugged her. "Then why do this for me?"

"I can see in your eyes how much you enjoy it." She shrugged her thin shoulders and gave him a smug look. "Besides, it gets me all tingling, too."

"Good."

The logs were crackling in the hearth beside them, and she was flat on her back on top of the comforter. His hands had explored her entire body, and at last she'd raised her knees and spread them apart inviting his attention. Like a serpent, his palm ran over her small mound of pubic hair and his finger found the moist source. He probed her to the second knuckle, and she clutched his hand and nodded her head for him to start.

He shed boots, outer clothes, and underwear in record time, and moved between her snowy legs, and she lifted her butt off the comforter to receive him. A cry came from her when he plunged inside her, and his hips began to ache to poke her into the tile floor.

Sweat soon lubricated his muscle-corded belly rubbing on hers as they struggled for an end—a giant display of fireworks to shower down on them. Their breathing became shorter and more labored. She clutched him, wild with her possession and pleasure's fast song.

Then, with a gurgling in his throat, he began to arch his back to drive the hard-rock spear deep into her contractions.

And she made a nasal sound that met his explosion inside her, and they collapsed in a pile.

She fought the hair back from her face with her fingers and blinked her dazed-looking eyes. "Don't leave me. Don't ever leave me, Slocum."

"I won't—tonight," he promised.

But he did leave her asleep the next morning before sunup. He hurried down the frost-glazed streets to a small café. After breakfast, he rented a livery horse and rode south down the Camino Real.

How long would she have lasted on that flat prairie country being his wife? A week, not more than two, and by then she'd have worn out every deck of cards on the ranch playing cards with herself. Then, she'd have to go to town—not to shop, but to beat a few good old boys at poker. Then, she'd be satisfied to go back to the ranch. Then, the next week, she'd be begging to go back again, and then, every day it would be an issue.

He rode south and threw her kiss. *Mary, I love you, but you ain't meant for that kind of a life. Keep dealing cards and raking in the money.* Somehow, he needed her name off that Wells Fargo list—he'd figure a way to do that.

19

Slocum sat cross-legged on the rise under a mesquite tree and scoped the Moores' farmhouse. There were dried yellow corn stalks all stacked up and several stacks of alfalfa hay. Moore milked several cows, and with his wife had gone to the barn early that day armed with milk pails. The dairy stock made lots of noise and filed in and out of the barn when he called for them. No sign of the road agent.

If Slocum wanted to, he could shoot One-Eye on sight and collect his pay. Wells Fargo would consider it fine with them—just so the bastard didn't come back and rob another shipment of theirs. But Slocum wasn't their executioner. They could hire someone else for that job.

The morning passed and no One-Eye. Moore even drove off to town with his milk. And she did the washing and hung it on the line. This far south, the day warmed up fast, and his spot on the hill overlooking the irrigated farm was not that cold to begin with. With no luck by late afternoon, he rode back to town and told the liveryman that he wanted to rent the bay horse the next day.

He found a cantina, and soon was drinking what the bartender called the coldest beer in New Mexico. Lukewarm was what he considered it. Maybe that was as cold as it got this far south. He talked to the small Mexican man for a while, and learned about some woman One-Eye Davis was seeing. Her name was Gonzales and she lived near the pueblo. That didn't make much sense because pueblos were all over New Mexico. But for two silver dollars he found out she lived north of town, and the bartender's mind became much clearer and he drew Slocum a map to her location.

It was too late for him to wander around in the dark and risk getting bitten by dogs, so he went and found supper, then slept in his bedroll in the livery. Before sunup, he had the Gonzales place in view. In the corral, he found a horse with saddle scars on his withers, and he felt better. The area between the corral and the jacal was open, bare ground.

In the soft purple light, he crossed it, and his heart beat hard when he stopped at the side of the front door. Using his pistol butt, he pounded on the door and then stepped aside—in case.

"Who is there? Who is there?"

"The sheriff," Slocum shouted. "And my men are all around the house. All of you come out hands high or we'll open fire on you."

"What should we do?" the woman inside asked.

"That ain't the sheriff. He's Mexican. That's some fucking bounty hunter. Stay down."

I'll show him a fucking bounty man! Slocum cocked his six-gun, then used his boot to smash the door open and rushed inside. One-Eye whirled around with a gun in hand and Slocum shot him. The outlaw's pistol rolled over in his fingers. His knees buckled. The woman screamed and fainted. One-Eye fell facedown.

Slocum moved around him, picked up his pistol, which was lying on the floor, and stepped over her. There were Wells Fargo canvas sacks in a pile in the corner—all empty. He went back to where the woman was sitting up on her butt looking woozy-eyed in the gun smoke's haze.

"Where's the money and gold?"

"He don't have any—"

Slocum holstered the gun in his belt and put his hands on his hips. "Lady, I'll start by cutting your right ear off if you don't start telling me where it went."

"Please don't hurt me." The chunky woman in her thirties held up her hands. "There is some hid in here. I don't know where he hid the rest."

"Start sacking it."

"Shouldn't we get a doctor for him?"

"Where's all this gold at?"

"The bars are buried. Some of the money is in here."

"Start sacking it. I'll see if he's alive."

"Who—who are you?"

"The fucking bounty man, I guess. He'd surrendered, he wouldn't have been shot." Slocum shook his head in disgust. He knelt down and rolled One-Eye over. He moaned.

"Oh, thank God, he's still alive," the woman said.

"Load the money and be quick."

"I-I know you—you and that fancy bitch," One-Eye said, and then put his hand to his shoulder. "You shot me."

"Right. Since you're going to live, where is all this loot you took?"

"I don't have it."

"I'll find it and after I do and dig it up, then you'll get a doctor's care."

One-Eye sat up wincing at the pain and looking at all the blood on his hand from holding the wound. "The gold's buried in the backyard. That damn stuff's impossible to sell."

"I'm going to take you and her to town. Get a doc to patch you up. First show me where to dig for it." He jerked the struggling One-Eye to his feet by his collar and shoved him to the doorway. "Come on, you're going, too," he said to the woman.

"What about all this money?"

"I'll come back and get it. Come on." They went out the back way, and he closed the doors. He caught up with them in the middle of the yard.

"Where's it buried under?"

"Under that old cart," One-Eye said.

"It better be there."

"It is."

"I'm telling you it better all be there."

He saddled the horse, loaded One-Eye in the saddle, and then the woman on behind him. "Don't let him fall off," he told her.

On his livery horse, he led the way back to a doctor's office, and left One-Eye to be patched, with orders that neither of them were to leave the office until he came for them. After he left them there, he went and telegraphed Thorpe to come down to Bernallio. He had the ringleader and some of the loot. He also left a sealed envelope for Thorpe at the telegraph office with directions in it to the Gonzales house.

Then he found some men hanging around a general store who wanted work. He charged six shovels and two picks to Wells Fargo and sent the men hiking to her place. Next, he swung by the doctor's office and learned that the bullet was out and One-Eye was bandaged.

He took One-Eye and the woman back to her house, passing the men Slocum had hired walking on the road. They looked puzzled at One-Eye and waved to him.

"See you up there," he said, and they agreed.

"What will you do with us?" she asked when they had left the men behind.

"Collect the bounty. I'm a fucking bounty hunter."

She shook her head in disapproval as she rode behind the outlaw.

At the jacal, he put most of his workers to digging. Two of the six were refilling canvas bags with the coins and money that she'd shown him were in the house.

In thirty minutes, he heard shouts outside. They'd found the gold. So he went out there and told them to start packing it into the house. One thing he began to realize as the loot was located. One-Eye had gotten enough loot from the robberies to worry Wells Fargo to death.

Soon, the money was tied shut in the canvas bags, which were put all in a stack. The gold bars were piled in the center of the floor. He gave each worker five dollars, told them they could keep all the shovels and picks, and swore them to secrecy. One-Eye lay on the bed. The woman tended to him, and every time he moaned, she gave him another spoonful of laudanum.

At dark, a wagon drove up and several men in canvas overcoats with shotguns arrived and jumped off the rig. Slocum wondered who they were, and met them with his rifle ready at the front door. "Hold it there. What's your business here?"

"You must be Slocum. I am George Steele. Dan Thorpe is on his way and wanted to be sure you had the backing you might need." He showed him the Wells Fargo badge and a deputy U.S. marshal badge as well. Steele was trying to see past him.

"Who are those others?" Slocum asked.

"Employees of Wells Fargo, sir. How much have you recovered if I may ask?"

Slocum held his hand up to stop them. "First, I want the woman released, she had no part in this. One-Eye Davis used her. I shot him today when he offered resistance and a doctor treated his wounds. He is full of painkiller now, but he cooperated with the recovery of the loot."

"How much did you recover?"

Slocum blocked the door. "Well?"

"We won't prosecute her and we will consider his helping you as cooperating with us."

Slocum stepped back and, filing in the room, they all looked shocked at the loot.

"Load it," Steele said, and they set down their arms to obey his orders. "You count it?" he asked Slocum.

"No way, but I think all there is left is right here."

Steele looked amazed as they made trip after trip out to the wagon. "He was responsible for more robberies than we even thought."

"Him, a kid, and an old drunk. And I guess he never let them have much of it so they wouldn't be seen spending it and draw attention."

"Probably. You looking for work?"

"No, sir. But you owe the livery for a horse, and Akins General Store for the shovels and picks. I was out thirty dollars for the labor, and I have some more bills I want paid."

"I'll pay the livery and horse bill and the rest. What else?"

Slocum nodded. "Now, there's reward money on this money and gold?"

"Yes, there is a ten-percent recovery reward. Where should I send it?"

"Don't send it. You take it to Mary Murphy. She's a card dealer in the Guadalupe Saloon and Gambling Hall in Santa Fe on the plaza. I also want her name off your wanted list. That embezzlement charge against her was trumped up."

For a moment, Steele looked like he'd blow up. Then it all faded. "All right, she's coming off the list."

"Notify everyone she's not wanted."

"Done deal—I can't believe you recovered all this loot."

"You make damn sure she gets off the list and gets this reward."

"I will. Why?"

"I owe her."

Steele accepted his words. "Where will you go next?"

"There's one more bunch of outlaws I want to see behind bars or dead."

"Tell me how I can help you get them. You can have whatever you want."

"Thorpe's been covering my bills so far. You can't ride in and arrest them. I'll figure out a way to get them."

Steele nodded his head. "I'd hire you in a minute."

"No news stories, no mention of my name?"

"That's a deal." Steel shook his hand and then turned to the man who had told him all the loot was loaded. "Get One-Eye Davis over there and load him, too."

"Yes, sir."

Steele touched his expensive hat. "Mary Murphy, huh? Interesting-sounding name. She expecting it?"

"No." It would sure knock her over, too, getting that much money. He wished he could see her face when Steele showed her how much she was getting.

"What will happen to him?" the woman asked in a small voice behind Slocum.

The wagon was gone in the night and One-Eye with it. Slocum turned in the doorway. "He'll do time in prison."

"Why did you save me?"

"You're no stage robber."

"No." She wrapped her arms around him and began to cry. "Oh, I thank you so much."

"Do you have any food?"

She looked up at him and blinked her wet lashes. "I have food."

"Let's eat it." He put his arm on her shoulder to comfort her.

Over the meal of beans and tortillas, he told her to sell One-Eye's horse and saddle, that he wouldn't need them and it would give her some money. She agreed that she would, then began lighting a new candle in a bottle.

"Where will you sleep tonight?" she asked.

"In town at the livery."

"Oh, stay here tonight and hold me. It has been a very tiring day."

He considered her for a moment with her bean burrito in his hand, and then he nodded—she was a little on the chunky side, but she was real. Besides, he still had half an erection from her hugging on him.

20

He reached Española and stepped off the stage in the light of dawn. His past night had been spent in the rocking, bouncing coach. It was a long ways from the night before when he had bounced on top of Señora Gonzales's belly and listened with a smile to her moaning in pleasure's arms. He slept little either night, but one was pure fun, the other real torture.

He left his gear at the stage office and went to the livery to get a horse. He could pick up Heck at the Flores Station, then be on his way north. The full moon would be coming soon, and May would be up there expecting him. So far, things were falling in place.

He was waiting for the passage of a double freight wagon when someone called to him.

"Slocum. Slocum." It was Bledstone. He came on the run and fell in beside Slocum, looking around to see if anyone would hear him. "You got One-Eye and the loot, too."

"The loot was extra."

"How much you get for it?" Bledstone hissed.

"I gave that to charity."

"Hey, I thought—"

"Listen, I caught the Kid, the old man, and One-Eye. All I know you did was fuck his girlfriend."

"All right. All right. But we're including your partner in on the reward. How much did you give away?"

"Bledstone, I ain't sure." Slocum looked hard across the street at an attractive Hispanic woman going down the stone walk and disappearing into a dress shop. He wanted rid of Bledstone. His presence grew harder and harder for Slocum to stand. "It don't matter, it's gone. I'm going up there to investigate the Boosters. When I get set to arrest them, I'll wire you. Where will you be?"

"Pagosa, I guess."

Slocum scowled at the man. He'd not learned his lesson, he might never learn it. "Booster catches you up there, he'll cut your throat," Slocum said.

"I'll plug him full of lead."

"If you get the chance."

"All right, I can stay here. You wire me first thing. I want to be in on it."

"You turn in your expenses?"

"Yes. Thorpe said we'd have it and our reward money in ten days."

"Collect mine. You can give Collie Bill his and mine."

Bledstone blinked at him in disbelief. "You giving that away, too?"

"That ain't any of your damn business."

Slocum stopped. Why ride a livery horse up there? Hell, Wells Fargo would pay his stage fare. He was taking the next stage north and not sharing it with this slob.

"What's wrong?" Bledstone asked.

"I've changed my mind."

"You want me to hold your share?"

"No, give it to Collie Bill. I'm getting me a room and sleep a couple of hours. See you."

He left him and went to the Alhambra. The room faced the south and was sun-warmed. Once under the covers, he slept till dark, and then went out and checked the stage schedule. The next northbound came in at nine, and would be at the Flores stage stop the next day at noon. Good. He got his ticket and went out to eat. The temperature was cooling after a warm day.

He started across the main street. The sun had fallen behind the western range of mountains and twilight spread over the street, which was choked with rigs, wagons, buggies, and mule teams. Amid all the traffic, whips cracking, and loud cursing, he crossed to the far side. From the corner of his eye, he spotted a face that blinked upon seeing him and then was gone.

Who was it? A man with as many enemies as he had had to know these things. The space between the saloon and the next store was empty when he reached it. He eased his way down through that space, which forced him to walk sideways toward the alley at the other end.

Near the exit, he could hear an out-of-breath person saying, "It's him all right," then huffing for breath. For a second Slocum wondered who was there. Never mind, they were talking about him.

"Damned if I know. But I saw him just now out there on Main."

"We better tell Harvey."

"Tell him what?" Slocum asked, and stepped out with his gun in hand. He knew neither of them. One was dressed in overalls and the other in dirty patched pants. They looked like riffraff. They were whiskered, unbathed, and their greasy hair stuck out in tufts.

"Ah, ah, nothing. Who are you?" Overalls asked. He looked to be in his thirties and was maybe the smarter one of the two.

"You boys appear to me to have my name on the top of your list."

The shorter one looked hard at his partner for an answer. Then they both broke and ran away screaming down the dark alley. "He's gonna shoot us! He's gonna shoot us!"

Slocum shook his head. They worked for Ryan. But if he wanted assassins, he'd better hire someone smarter. If Slocum weren't leaving on the stage in a few hours, he'd go and find the SOB and make a real believer out of him. But there was no time for that.

He boarded the stage at eight forty-five, and left for Flores Station in the chilly night. The canvas side curtains on the coach were tied down, but the cold had no problem going around them. Slocum wore his coat and had two woolen blankets to cover up with. A heavyset woman had a shawl she was wrapped up in. In her thirties, she looked like someone's wife. She nodded and gave a big smile to him when she squeezed with some effort through the door into the coach. Her cheap perfume was strong and her musk was stronger.

The third passenger was a small Mexican man who bundled himself up in a thick hand-woven cotton blanket in the rear seat, mumbling, *"Frio. Frio."*

He got off at Herman. The big woman slept some with her head on Slocum's shoulder. She also snored, so he ended up with his arms around her large girth and both of them under his blankets being tossed about in the dark coach. It was not paradise, and between her bad perfume and strong body odors, he was awakened several times wondering where in the hell he was at. At midnight, there was falling snow when they climbed down to relieve themselves in the stinking facilities out back of a stage stop. The coffee there tasted like tar. Even Erma found it bad-tasting.

Then Ute, the lanky driver, announced it was time to go, and they left the half-warm room for the cold outdoors and the wet flakes that melted on Slocum's face. Erma waddled from side to side going back, and then strained to pull herself up and inside. He put his hand on one of her large hams and gave her a good push to speed up the process and get her in. She giggled, and he regretted doing it.

They were off with fresh horses, and he and Erma were alone back on the front bench under his blankets.

"What'cha do fur a living, honey?" She'd already asked if he was married, had ever been, or had any plans for marriage.

"About anything that won't get me cross with the law and makes money," he answered.

"Well, honey, what you needs is a good woman to cook your meals and keep you occupied till next spring."

Her head resting on his chest, she hugged him like he belonged to her. "And I know just the one."

"Who?" He didn't really want to know who she'd suggest— probably her.

"My oldest girl Margarie."

"How old is she?"

"Ain't no never mind, she's old enough and she'd care for you well this winter. She ain't bad-looking. She ain't lazy either. Got a nice girlie figure like men like. And she can bust wood with any man."

"Why, hell, she can surely find herself a man up there in Colorado."

"You don't understand, mister. She found one and when he got her with child, he took his ass on down the road. They said he was already married back home somewheres anyhow."

"When's she due?"

"Oh, four months or so."

"She could still find a man."

"Yeah, but you're more respectable than most of them honyockers hanging around up there. I always wanted my girls to marry them a real respectable man."

"You marry one?"

"Lord, no, I married some old donkey dick. Man, I thought he was cute."

"He still around?"

"Naw, he got killed and I've had four others about that worthless. I just come back from settling the last one's family estate in Texas. He died two years ago."

"A large estate?"

"I ain't that rich and I put up with him till he died. I deserved something for that."

"You did. What killed him?"

"He was a lunger. You know, spit up blood and pieces of his lungs till he died."

"You must be an angel of mercy."

She giggled and reached for the crotch of his pants. "I'm a big one, ain't I?" she said. "It wasn't so damn cold and we had a little more room, I'd sure show you some mercy."

Thank God for cold weather.

21

The snow quit before daylight and there was only a skiff around, but colder weather had shut it down at the next stage stop. When he stuck his head out of the coach door, the first blast nearly took his hat.

"Whew, Erma, watch the wind."

She laughed, starting out after him. "Take a tornado to get me. Hellfire, there is one."

They both fought their way to the front door and spilled inside, grateful to be out of it. Ute joined them, jerking off his gloves and holding his hands out to the fireplace's heat. "You ain't got far to go?" he asked Slocum.

"No, and I'm glad."

"Your cowboy friend's sure helping Juanita. She needed someone when her husband got killed."

"Good."

"I can't blame him either. She's a pretty woman and the best damn cook on this run."

Slocum looked around to see if any of the Booster bunch was in the room, and then he agreed. His mind was more on May and the cabin. He was three days from getting up there, barring a heavy snow. She might not even be up there yet.

He wouldn't know until he got there. At first, he'd worried that it might have been a trick she planned to play on him, but after the night on the road they'd spent in his bedroll, he figured she'd be there.

At midday, they reached the Flores Station, and he unloaded his saddle and gear out of the boot. Rudy, one of the hostlers, helped him pack it inside out of the wind.

"Where's Collie Bill?" he asked the youth while walking back to the station.

"Went after an elk yesterday."

"He's not back?"

Rudy shook his head as they went inside, and then he took a seat on a wall bench to be out of the way.

Strange he'd gone off, Slocum thought. Erma was talking to Juanita, who brightened at the sight of him. "You're back?"

"Yes. Collie Bill is gone?"

"Just for a few days, he's elk hunting. We're about out of meat."

"Everything going all right?" He could read the lingering sadness in her eyes.

"Thanks to him. He's a good man. The boys who work for us like him." She looked at the pegged floor. "I'd never have made it without him."

He hugged her shoulder. "We ain't had any real food since we left home."

"Well, let's eat some."

"Amen," Ute said, already seated and ready.

After the meal, Ute shook Slocum's hand, and Slocum even hugged Erma good-bye. Her perfume and aroma still lingered. The stage left in the heatless sun of midday. Slocum went to the corrals and checked on Heck. The buckskin gelding was fine, and had put on a pound or two eating alfalfa hay that he might lose while on the move the next few days. By sundown, Collie Bill still wasn't back, and Juanita assured Slocum he was up at some hunting camp west of there.

Slocum made plans to ride out in the morning with one packhorse. He explained to Juanita while sitting across from her at the long table that he needed to scout some things. He finally got around to asking her about Perla.

"Oh, she is fine. Such a shame. She may never get over all that has happened."

He agreed. It was all branded in her mind. The death of her husband and the rape. But he needed some evidence that the gang was in on at least one of the stage robberies—that meant that Wells Fargo would move in. The shakedown of ranchers would be hard to prove, and with no one willing to be a witness against them, it meant any good lawyer would only laugh at the charges in court.

He should have gotten One-Eye to implicate them. No, he needed to prove they'd robbed a stage. Maybe after his meeting with May, he would know something besides how much he liked her and hot springs. He turned in early and woke early.

Rudy was up in the cold dark. The boy helped him saddle Heck and pack the bay. Juanita was up, too, making him a special breakfast and acting like a mother.

Where was he headed? Why? And for how long?

"A week, ten days, and I'll be back. Bledstone is bringing our money. Collie Bill gets a third."

"That's nice of you since he's been up here helping me."

He reached over and squeezed her hands. "I knew that and you needed him. He was in on this business from the start."

"I sent him hunting."

"Oh?" He buttered a freshly made biscuit.

"He needs to be sure he wants to stay here. I feel there is something pulling on him."

Slocum agreed and listened.

"I want him happy. I want him to stay if he wants to stay."

"Tough deal."

"Slocum, you know I need him, but not if he would be unhappy."

"Maybe he'll find an answer."

Her long dark lashes narrowed. "What if my friend Perla wanted you to stay with her?"

He dropped his chin and shook his head. "I couldn't. Besides, she is afraid to let anyone get close to her."

"Yes. You be careful. Sims is a mean, mean man."

"He ever bother you?"

She shook her head—but he knew that was a lie. She lied so he wouldn't go after Sims because of her. He knew her purpose even before her head shook. He gazed into her large doe eyes and sculptured face. Collie Bill better decide for her—it might be his last chance at a real life.

When Slocum was outside and mounted, his breath came in clouds. He thanked the boy for helping him and rode off leading the packhorse. The cold wind was cutting his cheeks and he pulled up the kerchief like a mask. Damn, it was cold. Those hot springs better be warm. The notion of May's subtle body and the swirling hot water made the entire effort sound worthwhile. Especially when he still smelled traces of Erma's sour scent. He tried hard to forget her.

At mid-afternoon, he finally reached the Crow Creek Stage Station. With a canvas pail, he watered the two horses, and then put a nose bag of corn over their heads before he went inside.

The bearded man standing inside the dining hall nodded in approval at him. "You're a real horseman, I can see that about yeah. Not many men'd draw water from a well before they came in to warm up."

Slocum stripped off his gloves. "First things first."

"Where you headed?"

"Colorado, if the road goes there."

The man went over and spit his tobacco in a brass spittoon. After wiping his whiskered mouth on the back of his hand, he nodded. "It still goes there."

"You want some coffee?" a gray-headed woman asked from the side door.

"Yes, ma'am." He had his coat unbuttoned, and the warmth of the room was almost more than he could stand.

"Guess you've got business up there?"

"I hope so," he said, and thanked her for the steaming cup.

"Lots of road agents. 'Course I'd bet they're all too lazy to bother anyone on a cold day like this."

Slocum blew on his coffee to cool it some. "I hope so."

"You're welcome to stay the night, ain't many hotels between here and there."

"Thanks, I can't, but I'd like something to eat, then I'll be on my way."

The old man nodded and then shouted, "Ruth, he wants to eat."

She stuck her face out of the side room. "I could tell that without asking."

The old man shook his head ruefully at Slocum. "You got a woman?"

"No."

"They're damn hard to put up with—at times."

Slocum agreed.

The sun hung low, and he knew he might regret having left the stage stop so late in the short day. He was trotting Heck through the tall timber on the two wagon ruts and looking for the features that May had mentioned. The cabin was farther up there than he'd expected. No need to be too concerned. He could stop, build a fire, and keep it going till sunup, but that would be a long night without May squirming underneath him.

In the twilight, he dropped into a wide-open grassy valley and could see the stream. This would be more like cow country, and somewhere upstream the ribbon of water contained May's hot springs. Then the smell of wood smoke reached his nostrils. He pushed Heck on, feeling certain he was close to finding her.

He rode up to the cabin with the light in the window. Stiff, he dropped to his sea legs and pulled down the crotch of his pants. Standing for a minute, he saw the door open and May rushed out putting on her coat.

"I'd about given up on you," she said, out of breath. "Put your pack stuff inside. Then we can take the horses up to the corrals."

They undid the diamond hitch, her on one side, him on the other. When the ropes were undone, he flipped off the canvas, and she took it to fold while he tossed the bedroll inside the toasty cabin and went back for the panniers. When he had the last one inside, he had to hurry to catch up with her leading the horses to the corral and shed.

"How have you been?" he asked, taking the leads.

"My brother Cal is dead," she said, sounding sad.

"Oh."

"Someone gut-shot him up in Pagosa. We ain't sure who done it. Rip may know and ain't telling me, too."

"I'm sorry." Bledstone's bullet had found its mark.

"I been some sad about it, but I wasn't going to let it ruin us having some fun."

"I'll try to liven things up."

She swung on his arm. "I am counting on you."

"You ever doubt I'd come?"

"Sure. I mean, some dumb old ranch girl invites a guy like you to an old line shack in hell and cold gone. What chance did I have?"

"But you came up here anyway?"

"I've spent my winters up here alone since I was fifteen. That bunch at the ranch gets pretty tough stuck in the ranch house and with nothing to do. Besides, I had no privacy. They haul up two ricks of hay up here each year for my horses. I probably have three loads stacked in the shed. During the summer, a hired crew of Mexicans comes up here and cuts me enough firewood for two winters."

"So in the winter you become a hermit."

"Sort of. When it's nice, I hunt and fish. Gets bad outside, I read books and write in my journal."

"What do you write?"

"Oh, nothing."

He opened the cabin and let her inside. "You can read some to me later."

"I'll think on it."

She shrugged off her jacket and let it drop to the floor. Then, looking up at him in the flickering light, she smiled. "It might be all about you."

He let his coat hit the floor and swept her up in his arms. Their mouths closed on each other and the heat of her tongue drove the cold out of him. He clasped her to him and his head whirled in abandonment—all the way up there he'd thought about this moment—the kindling of a fire.

Feverishly, she was ripping open his belt and pants between them. "I've waited and waited and waited for this—"

He smiled down at her as his pants fell to his knees. He bent over and shed his boots, standing on one foot, then the other. Her hand was familiarly feeling his crotch as she twisted back and forth like a thick drape in the wind. He shoved down her skirt and found she wore no underwear. Then she unbuttoned his long handles to get at him. He removed her flannel shirt and felt her pear-shaped breasts. His anxiousness increased when she clutched his dick and began to gently pump on it.

She wet her lips and looked up at him. "May I?"

He nodded, and his heart stopped as she went to her knees before him and took the head in her lips.

The door flew open and a voice of rage exploded his dream. It was Sims screaming and the lights went out.

He awoke lying facedown on the floor. His naked body shivering, he tried to clear his fuzzy vision. Where was she? Holding his pounding head, he rose in the darkness. The damn door stood wide open. Lucky he didn't freeze to death. He slammed it shut. Where was May?

Shaking from the cold, he fumbled with a match to light the candle on the table. Once it was lit, he raised the bottle the light was stuck in to search for her. If that no-account had hurt her—had done a damn thing . . . His giant shadow cast on the wall, he went around the bed and found May naked, crumpled on the floor.

He dropped to his knees and set the lamp aside. Gently, he lifted her cold naked body in his arms and laid her on the bed. Was she even alive? He put his ear to her lips.

She was still breathing. He wrapped her in the blankets, and then he went over and stoked the dying coals in the fireplace. It needed fuel. The wood was burned down. He piled split logs in the hearth and swallowed hard. Damn, he hugged his arms around his chilled skin. It was cold. Sims must have tried to beat his head to pieces. It was sore to the core. What now? He quickly dressed and then went over to see what else he could do for her.

She needed to be warmed up. If he knew how far away the hot springs were, perhaps he could carry her there. He shivered the whole time despite the radiant heat from the blazing fire. Even dressed and pulling on his boots, he still shook with the cold.

How long had Sims been gone? No telling. What had he done to her? Slocum could only imagine as he tucked his shirt in and looked close at her. She was breathing, but her skin felt like ice. Maybe if he crawled in and held her, he could warm her up some. His boots off, he climbed in the bed and wrapped her in his arms.

His heart quickened when she moved. *Warm up, gal. Don't freeze to death on me.* He kissed her cold forehead and then held her close. His own body was still trembling in waves. He clenched his teeth to stop them from chattering.

"Slo-c-c-cum?"

"It's me, baby. Save your strength. I've got to get you warm."

"Take—your—clothes off."

"I will." He shed his pants and kicked them out from under the covers; then he raised up and took off his shirt. Unbuttoning his underwear, he stripped it off his shoulder, lay down, raised his butt, and shed it.

Her skin was cold against his as he hugged and rocked her. "I'm sorry, May. I never knew he was following me."

"He wasn't. He came for me—"

"Save your strength."

"He shot Rip. He said he killed him. Rip was the only reason he never touched me—before." She began to sob and cry. "He killed Rip on account of me."

Her wet tears spilled on his chest. "When I wouldn't go away with him, he started slapping me. My mouth's cut inside. My teeth hurt. And I'm c-o-old."

With a shake of his head, he rocked her in his arms.

"Did he hit you?"

"Yes, when I wouldn't respond to him. After that, I-I don't remember a thing until you woke me."

"I guess he's gone. I bolted the door."

"Oh, I don't know if I can stand my other brother being dead, too—oh, Slocum hold me tighter. I'll get underneath you and we can be joined. That might warm me faster. I really need you close."

He moved to obey and, on top of her, he slipped his half-filled erection in her. Even her pussy was cold inside. "How far are the springs?"

"At the base of the hill."

"I'll carry you down there."

"No." She clutched him. "Not yet. I'm feeling warmer already."

So he made love to her slowly, and stopped for her seizures of shivering. They told him her body was trying to raise its own temperature. Her eyes began to come alive and she smiled behind her thickening lip. In the orange light, the bruises Sims'd given her began to show on her face. Her left eye looked swollen.

She raised her knees. "Now finish me."

In no time, he had her breathing hard and her heels spurring him on. Then he felt the explosion coming and buried his swollen dick in her. He came and she fainted.

"May? May, are you all right?"

"Fine," she said dreamily. "I'm even hot."

He got up, partially dressed, and fed the fire. Made some coffee and then slipped on his jacket to go check on the horses. When he discovered the gate lying down, his heart stopped. But he found the packhorse and another horse were standing in the shed. He went inside the dark shed and tossed them some fresh hay in the mangers. Sims must have stolen Heck.

He tied the gate in place and went back to the house. When he opened the door, he discovered May standing before the fire with a blanket over her head. She turned and waved him over. "Coffee's done."

"Good. He left us two horses, or they decided to come back to the hay."

"Good." She handed him her steaming cup, and looked up at him with her black eye. "I'll get another one."

She stepped daintily in her bare feet to the fireplace, and

bent over under her cloak to pour another. Back beside him again with her own cup, she hugged him, and her blanket slipped off her right shoulder so her breast was exposed. "Why did he have to ruin it?"

"What did he ruin?" Slocum switched hands with his coffee and gently fondled her breast to tease her. "I'm having fun."

She closed her eyes. "It's the only way I can even stand to think about going on living."

"Was he alone, do you think?"

"I guess. I never heard or saw anyone else."

"Do you need to ride down to the ranch and see if he told you the truth?"

She nodded. "I better tomorrow. I don't know if I can face it. He said he killed Rip."

"I understand."

With one hand, she clasped the blanket shut and rested her forehead on his chest. "I've never been good with men in my life. Oh, I've had some affairs—but that night in Pagosa in the hot springs was a dream come true to me. And I wanted this one to be another. Damn that blasted Sims for ruining it. Damn his alligator hide."

"You better get some rest. You'll be sore in the morning." He sipped some of his coffee.

"Why do I think this will be our last night together?"

"There's men looking for me. Two Kansas deputy sheriffs. They hear from some stage driver—'Oh, Slocum, he's up in Colorado. I seen him a week ago in Pagosa.' Or some drunk in a bar says, 'Slocum's in Santa Fe,' and they come looking."

"You could hide at our ranch. No one comes in we don't let in."

"It ain't that easy."

"Nothing's that easy, is it?"

He finished his cup and set it down. Then he swept her up in his arms and carried her to the bed. "You need some sleep."

She kissed him, but he could tell it hurt her sore mouth. When she was in the bed, he added her blanket on top of her and began to undress.

"How long would you have stayed up here?"

"A week or so and I'd get edgy." He rebuilt the fire for the night.

"Damn, I could have had the memory of that anyway."

In minutes, he was in bed and slid in beside her. She pulled him on top of her. "I may cry the whole damn time—but love me."

He agreed, and began to explore her naked body with his free hand running over her skin. Morning would come soon enough.

Sims, you better sleep well tonight wherever you're at. Your last damn days are numbered.

22

They parted in the frigid predawn. Slocum watched May ride off to the south to see about her brother's death, and he headed east to find Sims. Before noon, Slocum reached the Crow Creek Stage Station, and the bearded man told him that early that morning Sims had ridden south on his buckskin horse. Slocum knew the bay could not catch Heck if the big man pushed him, but after a cup of hot coffee and some cold biscuits, he set sail. Sooner or later, he'd find him—the man's time was running out.

By the early winter sundown, he was back at the Flores Stage Station. No sign of his buckskin horse in the corrals or around the yard in the twilight. Rudy came out and took his horse.

"Sims been here today?"

"No, Señor."

"Collie Bill back?" He motioned to the house.

"*Sí*. He killed a big elk, too."

"Thanks, Rudy." He took his bedroll and rifle off the bay and packed them to the stage building.

"Slocum!" Juanita came on the run when he stepped inside the warm room.

He dropped his things on the floor in a pile and swung her around.

"Hey there." Collie Bill came out of the kitchen. "Go easy there on the next Mrs. Hankins."

Slocum looked into her eyes. "Is that so?"

She nodded and hugged him. "Yes, he asked me this morning."

"Heard you killed a big elk." Slocum came across the room with his arm hugging her shoulder possessively. Damn lucky guy. Collie Bill'd make a good living at this place. And a real lady for a wife. He thought about May and her ranch—no way. He'd better stop dreaming.

"Learn anything?" Collie Bill asked.

"Word is out that Sims shot Rip Booster a couple of days ago. Cal's dead. Bledstone gut-shot him up in Pagosa and they buried him at the ranch. And besides Sims caving in my head with a gun butt, he also stole Heck."

"Where did you learn all that?" Collie Bill asked, sounding impressed.

Slocum winked at Juanita, then stepped over and took a seat on the bench opposite him. "A little bird told me in a line shack up north."

"Juanita said Bledstone was going to leave our part of the money here," Collie Bill told him.

Slocum frowned. "He didn't come through yet?"

"Not yet. You don't think he's took a powder on us?"

Slocum took off his felt hat and scratched his head. No telling about that worthless SOB. "If he has, I'll nail his hide to the shit-house door."

"You two better eat." Juanita brought them each a large flame-roasted elk steak covering a tin plate. "The trimmings are coming."

"She must be a *bruja*. How did she know I ain't ate in twenty-four hours?" Slocum asked, rolling up his sleeves.

"Hell, she looked in your eyes and seen how empty you were on the inside."

Slocum stopped cutting on his steak and looked over at him. "This is the best thing you've ever done."

"You'll have to wait and see."

"No, you came in this country on a borrowed horse, no job, no prospects for one."

"You set me up."

"No, you did all this."

"I thought about that the whole time I was up there hunting and staying in that line shack. You're right. This place and her is right for me."

"Good—" He paused. "Have you heard anything from Perla Peralta?"

"No, why?"

Juanita came in with more food, a big bowl of frijoles and fresh-made tortillas.

"You talked to the señora?" Slocum asked her.

"Not in a few days, why?" She frowned at him.

He stood up and forked a strip of steak in his mouth. "I need to ride up there and check on her. Sims ain't here, he might be up there. Loan me the roan horse."

"Sure. Stay here and finish your meal. I'll have Rudy saddle him." She shot a a look at Collie Bill.

"Take him," said Bill. "He needs a fast horse. Hey, I'll go along."

Juanita turned without another word, threw a cloak over her shoulders, and went out for the sheds.

"No, you stay here," Slocum said. "You've got a wife, two little kids, and a business to protect here."

"Yes, I do. Finish your meal." Collie Bill shook his head, looking concerned. "It's colder than blue blazes out there again tonight."

Slocum closed his eyes for a moment. The headache was back. Sims must have tried to cave his head in. The top of his skull felt sore as a boil. It would be late when he got up there. No matter so he wasn't too late.

Juanita came back in and told him the horse was saddled and ready. "Tell her to come see me when this is over," she said.

"I will. Thanks, sorry, I've got to run."

The two of them walked him outside. He thanked them, kissed Juanita on the cheek, and mounted the roan. Then, with a wave to them, he set out in a long trot under the stars for the Peralta Ranch. The full moon would be up in a short while so he'd have plenty of light.

He reached Perla's place before midnight. There was no

sign of his buckskin horse in the yard or anywhere he could see in the moonlight. A sleepy-voiced woman came to the front door when he knocked the second time.

"Yes, what is it?"

"My name is Slocum. I must talk to the señora."

"She is asleep."

"This is very important. I must talk to her tonight."

"She is asleep. It is late."

"Carla, who is out there?" It was Perla's voice.

"A man named Slocum. He says he must talk to you— tonight."

"Show him in and I will go put on my robe. Show him some kindness. He is a very strong man and must have a good reason to get us up."

"Sí, señora." The door opened wider and Carla admitted him. "Follow me. The señora will be down in a few minutes." After closing and bolting the great doors, she showed him by candle lamp to the large dining table in a room off the foyer entrance and past the dark grand staircase he remembered.

She left the lamp on the table and went to let down the overhead light. She lit some of the candles, then hoisted it back up. It shed a soft light in the room. Then she went across to the hearth and stirred the ashes in the fireplace and put new wood on it.

After she rose with some effort, she looked over at him. "You can warm yourself by this fire."

"Sí. Gracias."

With a nod, she vanished out the doorway, in her tightly bound old robe, her slippers softly slapping the tile floor. He unbuttoned his coat and removed it. The fireplace was too inviting. He crossed over and warmed his hands. When Perla cleared her throat behind him, he turned and nodded.

"Good evening."

She nodded. "Is something wrong?"

For a long moment, he looked at her. Her beauty roiled his guts. She was straight-backed, wrapped in a thick white robe, and her smooth coffee complexion shone under the light. But she hadn't come down for his appraisal of her looks.

"There have been some things changed in the past week.

Both of the Booster brothers are dead. So that's maybe the good news. Cal was shot over a week ago in Pagosa in an attempt to assassinate someone. Sims shot Rip and killed him at the ranch, by my information."

She stood a few feet away from him as the flames began to lick the wood. "Will Sims run things now?"

"No, he's a fugitive and on the run. I feared he might have come by here."

"That was very thoughtful of you to come and tell me this, but we have seen nothing of him."

"He's here. I mean, I think he's close by."

"You think we are in danger?"

"Yes."

"There is little we can do until the sun comes up to check on this. Would you stay the night? It is late and I am certain you're tired. You must have came a long way."

"Thank you."

"Carla will show you to a room. In the morning, we can decide if he is around here. Thank you so much for coming, good night."

"Yes, ma'am."

He watched her leave the room. It was cold outside, but nothing like the temperature of the room after she left. It was an ice cave.

"Señor?" Carla asked from the doorway in a few minutes. "Have you eaten?"

"Yes. I'm fine."

"The señora was concerned. The room for you is in the back."

He slipped on his coat and hat. "I must put my horse up after you show me the room."

"I understand. This way."

They went through the kitchen, which smelled of onions and peppers. She showed him the bedroom down the hall. It was small, but had a large bed rather then a cot. After she lit a candle, she took him to the back door giving him instructions about the stables, and said she would wait for his return to let him in and relock the door.

He apologized to her for keeping her up and then he hurried

off. His boot soles crunched the frosty ground. The yard dogs accompanied him leading the horse, and en route one of the big males stopped stiff-legged and growled in the night.

What had he smelled or heard? Then they began to wag their tails again as if everything was all right, and they competed for his attention. The roan was put up in a stall and fed some hay. The barn was too dark to search for the grain. Slocum hurried back to the house.

Carla let him in and then relocked the door. Without a word, she went off into the dark house.

The bed was crisp and fresh when he turned back the cover. While he was at the corral putting up the roan, Carla had even kindled up the small fireplace. Feeling guilty, he climbed in under the covers. The bed was clean and he was about as bath-less as an old hog. But his conscience didn't keep him awake long. He soon fell asleep.

The sound of help stirring in the kitchen nearby awoke him. He dressed and sat on the edge of the fine goose-down bed to pull on his boots. He scrubbed his beard stubble in his cal-loused hands.

Maybe he'd misjudged something about the killer instinct in Sims. Why had the man left him alive? It made no sense. Sims came up to the line shack after May Booster like he thought she'd take up with him. Then, when she wouldn't, he beat her up and left. Of course, the man must have realized the setup that protected them was based on the Boosters' power and threat. When he shot Rip, he killed the source of that strength,

Slocum wiggled his right heel down in the second boot, clapped on his hat to cover his mussed-up hair, and headed for the door.

"Oh, good morning," one of the women said as she discov-ered him coming into the bustling kitchen. A full-bodied woman with a touch of gray in her hair was busy stirring a pot on the stove.

Eyes fluttered, hair was touched, and smiles were pasted on their curious faces, all with a large question written on their foreheads. Who was he?

"Good morning," he said. "My name's Slocum."

They nodded. A short girl in her late teens shook her fine butt across the tile floor to bring him a cup of coffee.

He thanked her and took a stool. The woman stirring the pot looked to be the boss.

"Fix him some *huevos*," she said, taking charge. "Nana, make him some tortillas."

He kept feeling the looks they stole to check him out. But the coffee was rich and smooth, and the shaking of their fannies to get the cooking going was interesting enough to admire.

"I see you have found my kitchen," Perla said, sweeping into the room. "Are they feeding you?"

"It's in the works," he said, and rose.

"Come. They can bring it in the dining room when it is ready." She strode ahead of him. The fringe on the divided riding skirt swished around her boots, and he enjoyed the view of the shapely leather-encased derriere. Her back was erect, and he wondered where she had learned to stand so tall.

She showed him the chair at the head of the table, and took the one on the right. A very proper seat for a visiting male. How polite of her, but she did few things wrong—just did everything stiffly. He considered her an iron rod.

He tossed his hat on the floor and quickly turned back to face her. "Sorry I woke you up last night, but I feared—"

"No need to apologize. I felt very safe last night. I am in your debt again, Slocum."

He shook his head. Her face, her mouth, and the movement of her hands entertained him. She could continue for hours. "No, but I want to be certain he doesn't come here and try something."

"Did an archangel send you?" The corners of her mouth showed her mild teasing amusement.

"Maybe—" The kitchen crew interrupted him and served them breakfast. They brought him some eggs and ham with frijoles and cheese and salsa burritos. They brought Perla two small cinnamon rolls. When the coffee cups were refilled, the crew retreated, and left Slocum and Perla alone in the sun-filled room.

"You were saying?" she asked.

"I don't know any archangels."

"But you came to my rescue before."

"Perla, I just happened to be there."

"Since you are my guest, may I interest you in a bath, a shave, and even a haircut?"

"It all sounds wonderful, but I'm not here to interfere."

Her brown eyes melted and she put her hand on his forearm. "Interfere with what? I am—I am so glad you're here I could cry. I did wrong sending you away. You offered me your protection. I was so afraid for myself I couldn't accept it. Now you have given me another chance."

"Chance?"

Her fingers squeezed has arm. "Yes, if you will stay, I'll accept your generous offer."

"I'm here."

"Now, we need to make arrangements." She looked at him appraisingly. "Yes, I think my husband's clothing would fit you. That doesn't matter, does it? He of course is deceased."

"Won't bother me a bit."

The woman in charge in the kitchen, Jolanda, cut his hair, to the critical comments of the four others. They looked closely at her work, some touching him and telling her what she should do. When she was finished, they filled a copper tub set up in his bedroom with buckets of steaming water, and demanded he throw all his clothing out in the hall. Then they laughed.

There were fresh clothes laid on the bed for him. He used the water till it turned tepid and let the pores soak. While the tub really was too small for him, he enjoyed the luxury of the moment. At last, he dried off and dressed, grateful for the fire in the hearth they'd built up for him.

Jolanda had promised to shave him after his bath, so when he was dressed, he went back to the kitchen.

Two of the girls giggled at the sight of him.

Before he could ask the point of their joke, Jolanda cut in. "Oh, we thought you might have dissolved like soap in that water."

"Not this time." They laughed.

When his face was smooth-shaven and tight from the alcohol aftershave she'd applied, he found Perla in the office working on her books. She set down her pen and twisted around in the swivel chair to look him over from head to foot. "No one would know you."

"I've wished that many times."

"I have no business asking you, but you are educated and a man of manners. You were not raised on some small farm."

He nodded. "The war changed all that."

"Ah, the war, it scarred many men. My husband fought in it. He came home and his wife was dead. His children, too. He tried to drink away his trouble. But he gave that up and came to Mexico City—I met him there. He was much older than me. My father was upset when he asked to marry me.

"He told my father he had a great hacienda in northern New Mexico. So my father sent a man with him to see this place. They did not return for two years. He wrote me many lovely letters and built this house in the meanwhile. So I came as his bride to this house with a real fountain that even my father's rich friends did not have in their houses."

"Your husband was Hispanic, too?"

She wrinkled her nose. "Some by the name, but his hair was blond and he had blue eyes. He would have passed for a gringo anywhere. His father was half and his mother was Irish. She might have been the second white woman in New Mexico. She, too, was a young bride to an older man who had buried two wives and four children. He was their only heir to survive."

Slocum held his hand up to the high ceiling. "He built all this in two years?"

"No, his father had started it, but he had never finished it." She laughed. "I can recall how worried I was down in Mexico City, about him and what I would move to—but when you are young, you can manage with less, huh?"

He nodded.

There was commotion in the kitchen. Perla rose and frowned. He did the same, and saw Jolanda come in the room drying her hands on a towel.

"Señora, Benny is here. He said this morning some men have stolen several of the mares from the herd."

"I am coming," Perla said.

"Count me in," said Slocum. "They may be leftover men from Booster gang taking anything they can sell."

In the kitchen, the young Mexican looked devastated, holding his sombrero in both hands. "I had no gun to stop them, Señora."

"You didn't need a gun. Which way did they go?"

"South, I think," he said.

"Why don't you stay here?" Slocum said to her. "I can handle them."

"I am not a child," she said sharply. "These are my horses."

Slocum nodded, and she turned away biting her lip as if in regret. "I know," he said, "and they are important to you, Perla. Send Benny along with me. He knows this country and can help me drive the horses back."

"What—what if—" She shook her head.

"They won't kill me."

"I can't ask you—"

"Can't ask me what?"

She rushed in and hugged him, buried her face in the starched shirt. "Slocum, I lost one man. A man like you who would have fought lions bare-handed for me. I—I can't let you."

He lifted her chin and looked into the wet eyes. "We'll be back with your mares. Keep an eye out. Sims may try to swing back by here and hurt you."

She swallowed and stepped back. "Sorry."

"No, we'll talk when I come back."

She fought the tears back and tried to recover her composure. "What do you need?"

"A packhorse with some food and a bedroll for *him*." He indicated Benny.

"We can have that ready in minutes," Jolanda said, and hurried off.

In twenty minutes, he and the quiet young man rode out. Benny led the way. The packhorse in tow, they headed southwest.

The heatless sun showed it was past noontime. That meant less than five hours till sundown, and the full moon wouldn't rise for some time after that.

Darkness might shut the rustlers down and they could overtake them. Those were the plans he shared with the quiet young man as they trotted their horses.

"Can you shoot a pistol?" Slocum asked him.

"*Sí*. I am not such a good aim."

Slocum laughed. "I have a loaded pistol in my saddlebags. You won't shoot me?"

"No, no."

"Good, you can have it when we stop again."

Benny nodded and they pushed on.

They took up the rustlers' tracks in the valley where the rest of the horses lifted up their heads at their approach.

"That is bad country they drove the mares into." Benny pointed to the hills ahead.

"Good, that will slow them down."

The young man nodded.

Later, they found several loose horses. Most were broodmares heavy with foals that had been abandoned.

"What can we do with them?" Benny asked.

"They'll go on home. Horses can find the way themselves."

He nodded, but his brown eyes looked concerned.

"They'll beat us back with the others. Don't worry."

Slocum motioned for him to move on. The trail was hot despite the weak sun and the cold. The tracks and horse apples went over a steep pass, and when the two men reached the top, Slocum saw some horses in the valley below. He held out his hand to stop Benny.

"Get back. They're down in this valley. I saw some of them. They've made a fire. They'll camp there."

"What should we do?"

"Stay out of sight till dark, then we'll sneak up and take them. They didn't expect anyone to take up their tracks this soon or they'd still be driving them."

Benny nodded, leading his horse and the packhorse back down the hill to a flat place where they hitched all three horses.

"How many are down there? I thought maybe four or five stole them."

"We can count 'em." Slocum dug out the telescope. They went back up and lay on their bellies on the ridge to view the rustlers. Slocum counted four. After a look through the glass, Benny agreed on the number.

"The full moon won't come up till late. They'll go to sleep. We'll sneak down and take them."

"They are bad hombres, no?"

"They won't be with a gun in their face."

"I was not there, I was with the horses when those *bandidos* raided the ranch. They raped my wife—"

"The señora told me who they were."

Benny nodded. "I have hated them for a long time for what they did to my Alicia. She has never been right since that day. Her mind is gone. It must have been very bad what they did to her."

"The Booster brothers are dead."

"Good. I hope it is very hot in hell for them."

"I agree. It has been very bad times. Benny, we better rest, it will be a long night."

"*Sí.*"

Darkness covered the land. A few stars sparkled in the cold sky. Rifle in his hand, Slocum led the way. From small pine to small pine, he moved using the side of his boots to get a foothold on the face of the slope. Whiffs of wood smoke reached his nose. He could stand a good fire to warm himself.

He glanced up as the small Mexican came after him. Benny was athletic, Slocum knew from how he could swing on a tall horse without a stirrup. Slocum's boot loosened some small rocks, and they rolled downhill as he stood still and listened, hoping not to wake the outlaws or warn them.

Their descent proved to be slow. When at last they were in the bottoms, they crossed the small frozen stream. The ice cracked under their weight. Slocum wondered if it might cave in, but soon they were across it and his heart beat slower.

The campfire was a hundred feet ahead. He sent Benny

toward the horses on the left so if one of the outlaws broke and ran, he would be covered. Then, with the rifle in his gloved hands, he stepped quietly through the grassy open space.

There were four humps under blankets in a circle around the fire. Two of them snored loudly. Slocum laid his rifle down, drew his Colt, and squatted by the first sleeper. He stuck a finger to the man's lips and put the gun muzzle in his face.

"Get up slow. No tricks. No sound," Slocum whispered.

The man obeyed and rose with his arms high. With him in view, Slocum did the same to the next one. He clapped his left hand over the man's protest.

"Shut up," Slocum hissed, and the wide-eyed older man obeyed and joined his buddy.

Benny came over and held the .44 on them.

"Huh?" the next one grunted, sitting up.

"Shut up. Get out here." Slocum saw him move under the covers and knew he had a pistol.

The .44 in Slocum's fist sent an orange flare out of the muzzle and made an ear-shattering blast. The man's shot was muffled by the blankets, and he fell back from the lead that struck his face like a thud on a watermelon. Slocum moved swiftly to the next man and kicked the gun he tried to produce from under his covers out of his hand.

"Get out here or die."

"I'm—I'm coming. Who the fuck are you, the damn law?"

"No," Slocum said. "We're the husbands of the women that you raped at the ranch."

"Aw, hell. We was just having fun."

"How would he know your wife?" Slocum asked Benny.

"They stole her necklace. It was made of hammered dimes."

The man who Slocum'd gotten out of bed last shook his head. "Not me."

Slocum looked at the other two for their answer. They shook their heads, too.

He and Benny tied their hands behind their backs and then their feet.

"We better see what they've got," Slocum said, and motioned to their things.

"We ain't got nothing. No one paid us our share," the outspoken one said.

"What's your name?" Slocum asked, on his knees reaching into the war bag.

"Ted."

"Who are the rest of you?"

"He's Myers and that's Peg on the end."

"Who's the dead man?"

"Larry Kent."

Something jingled as he felt around in the bag. Slocum stopped, and then reached in deeper. The small hammered coins on a chain hooked in his fingers came out into the rising moonlight.

"Benny, come over here."

He came and squatted. Then he carefully took the necklace, held it up in the campfire's light, and began to swear aloud in Spanish.

"I won that in a card game. Didn't I, boys? Didn't I?"

Slocum stood up. "I don't really care what you do with him," he told Benny.

"What did he do to her?" Benny asked Slocum.

"Ask him." Slocum gave a toss of his head toward Ted.

"What did you do to my Alicia?"

"I won that—I never—"

"Tell me. I must know."

"I didn't—"

"Give me your knife," Slocum said to Benny.

"What for? What you going to do to me?" Ted cried.

"Personally, I'd cut your sack open and stick your left leg through it. But right now, I'm going to notch your ear until you tell him." Slocum took hold of his ear as if ready to begin.

"Okay, okay. I was drunk. I can't remember much. We were raping them all."

"And—"

"And I guess I got a little rough—"

"How rough?"

"I might have slapped her a time or two. I don't remember much, except I couldn't get a load off. She wouldn't suck on it. I think I fucked her ass, too."

"Heard enough?" Slocum asked Benny.

"*Sí*. He makes me sick. I wish I could make him like she is."

"He ain't worth much."

Benny stuck the pistol in his waistband and hurried off into the night. It was time for a man with such a burden to be by himself. Slocum put more wood on the fire. The tongues of the flame licked at the night and he sat dry-eyed and looked at the three worthless rustlers. He wasn't a lyncher. He wouldn't make a good express man and executioner of every would-be stage robber either. But he could come close with these three. They'd ran roughshod over innocent people like Benny's Alicia, and God knows how many other small ranchers' wives had paid the tax. *Sons a bitches* . . .

23

It took all the next day to drive the horses back, and it was past dark when he reached the ranch with his three prisoners and the corpse of the fourth strapped over his horse. He rode in, leading the prisoners on their horses, and saw the buckskin horse in the starlight. Sims was there. Damn.

His heart stopped. He jerked the .44 out of the scabbard. "If one of you bastards move off your horses, when I find you I'll kill you."

He rushed to the house under the starlight and burst in the front door. Inside, he could see through the blue haze from a gunshot that someone was sprawled on his back on the floor at the base of the stairs. He was hatless, and his long curly black hair was spilled on the tile.

Seated on the stairs being comforted was Perla, with a smoking six-gun still in her hands. Jolanda and the house girls were crying and hugging her. Her glance met Slocum and her lips trembled when she tried to speak.

"I—I—told him to stop."

He reached up and took the gun from her limp hand. "You had no choice." He turned to her cook. "Jolanda, there are three rustlers and one dead one out there. Get the men to take them prisoner and lock them up for the sheriff."

"Yes," she said, nodding at him as he reached down and gently lifted Perla in his arms like she was a feather.

With the precious cargo at last in his arms, he couldn't glance away from her magnetic face. Under his rundown boots, the stairs were like clouds as he climbed them, consumed by her face and the rest of her beauty.

On the top floor, she said, "The second door."

He nodded, and pushed it in with a boot toe. The fireplace crackled and the orange light flooded the shadowy room. With his butt, he closed the door. Her small hands framed his face, and she raised up until her mouth was against his. Then, when they brushed lips, her arms flew around his neck and they plunged into a deep pool of hard breathing.

The world swirled around them. He undid her gown, then held her up and soon tasted her rock-hard nipples. She swept his face away to look at him and whispered, "The bed."

When she was on the sheet, he toed off his boots, dropped his gun belt, and shed his jacket and shirt while she undid the buttons on the gown down the front, exposing the orange-fired brown skin. He wanted to kiss every inch of it.

In minutes, they were in each other's arms and coupled in a dizzy head-whirling passion that put the whole world aside. His hands clasped her small rock-hard butt, and her contractions inside pulled the skin off his overinflated erection.

The explosion left them both trembling, but not ready to quit—not ever ready to stop. She was on top next, riding him, then on her hands and knees underneath him. They laughed, and then grew aroused again—consumed by each other's teasing into another tryst that took them to new heights.

He awoke hungover, sat up on the edge of the bed, and combed his hair through his fingers. Soon, she was pressing her breast into his shoulder. "Where do you go?"

"I need to see about my prisoners."

She slipped onto his lap and smiled up at him. "Once more."

He closed his eyes and nodded. How could he refuse such a woman?

Later, they lay in each other's arms.

"You will ride on?" she asked.

"It damn sure isn't you. I mean, the reason why I am leaving."

"I think I understand, but—"

He put a finger to her mouth and said, "I won't forget you."

"I agree."

"Agree to what?"

Like a cat, she rolled on top of him and sat up sweeping her hair back. "I think I have found myself. Never again will I be afraid. That was what you did for me."

"Good. Good."

She bent over and kissed him. "If I ever hear that you came by and did not stop here, I will track you down."

"I won't."

24

The sheriff in Española was a small Mexican who accepted the three prisoners and their handwritten signed confessions to rape, horse rustling, and cattle rustling. They claimed they'd never robbed a stage. That was Sims and others. Slocum had no argument with that—he left the courthouse after being assured they would stand trial and be sentenced when the circuit judge came by.

Then he rode out the road east, and in mid-morning stopped at Tonyah's jacal. She came sleepy-eyed to the door, half-wrapped in a blanket, and blinked at Slocum. Obviously, she was naked under the wrap. Her sausage leg was exposed almost to the lip of her belly.

"Where's Bledstone?" he asked

"I haven't seen him in days. He owes me money," she whined.

He shoved her aside and pushed the door open.

The bare-chested boy who bolted up in the bed let out a scream. "I didn't know she was your girl."

Slocum scowled at him. "She damn sure ain't mine." He turned back to her. "Where did he go?"

"Santa Fe—I don't know. Can I go back inside? It's cold out here."

"Sure." He walked over to Heck and checked the cinch. Maybe that no-account was down there and had probably already spent Slocum's and Collie Bill's money. A toe in the stirrup, then he swung up and rode off.

The day was probably done. In the west, the sun was sinking fast. Back in town, he'd get a room in the hotel and go on in the morning. That damn slob Bledstone had better count his days. They were damn sure going to be shorter if he ever caught him. Made him madder about the SOB taking his friend's money than it did *his* share. But Collie Bill had lovely Juanita and those two small kids of hers, plus a prosperous small ranch and stage station—still, the money would mean a lot to him.

Plus Sims and the Boosters were gone. He wondered about May. She had a ranch, she could figure out how to run it. Shame about her. She could have been lots of fun to have gone hot-water swimming with in another snowstorm.

Perla would take charge of her ranch and she would be fine. He dismounted at the livery to put Heck up.

"You're Slocum, ain't ya?" the white-whiskered old man asked when Slocum led Heck inside.

"Yeah." He started unthreading the latigos.

The old man looked around, then spit some tobacco aside. "Two Kansas deputies were in here not an hour ago. They was asking about you."

Slocum went to rethreading the leather. "Thanks. Where did they go?"

"Going to see the sheriff, they said. Maybe he knew where you were at."

Slocum paid him two silver dollars for his troubles, and the old man let him and Heck out the back door into the alley. He recalled Maria's sister, who lived a block or so away. Maybe he would stop there and get some sleep before he rode south.

The woman in her thirties, with a shawl on her shoulders, answered the door and recognized him in the twilight. "What can I do for you, Señor?"

"Do you have a man?"

"No." She frowned at him and checked her cleavage.

"I need to put my horse in back and sleep here for a few hours." He looked around in the twilight and saw nothing out of place. "I can pay you."

"No, no, you are the man who hit Ryan over the head and saved my sister Maria. Come in, Señor."

"Let me put the horse in back."

"Oh, *sí*. Are you hungry?"

He nodded. "Don't go to any trouble."

"I can find something."

When she closed the door, he led Heck around back and loosened the girth. He'd only be there for five hours or so, and then he had to hit the road. The buckskin would be fine hitched to the small mesquite tree for that long.

He used the rear door and stuck his head inside. "I'm coming in."

"Oh, I am making you some tortillas," she said, looking back at him in the light of the fireplace. On her knees, she was swirling the growing flour tortilla between her palms. The orange-red light danced on her face. Her cheekbones were too high and her mouth too thick for her to be pretty, but her smile was warm as if she was pleased he had chosen her casa.

He took off his hat and coat, and went over to squat close to her to absorb some of the heat. The one-room jacal was plain. There was a shrine on one wall where candles could be set, and a pallet on the floor. A steamer trunk sat to one side, and her Sunday dress hung on a hanger on the wall. Four hats, two of felt and two straw ones, were lined on pegs beside the back door. Her two small windows, one on front, one in back, were covered with small drapes. A louvered folding Chinese divider hid something in the far corner, and a single lighted candle in a bottle furnished the other light.

"How is Maria?" he asked.

"I have no idea. She left the next day." She rolled her lips inward as if about to cry. "I—I have heard nothing from her."

"Do you think that Ryan has her?"

"*Sí,* but there is nothing I can do. He is a powerful man, *patrón.*"

"Slocum's my name."

"Francisca is mine. I am sorry, Señor." A tear ran down her cheek. "There is nothing I can do. I fear for her safety."

"Is he down at the San Juan Mission village?'

"That is where he lives." She sniffed.

"You have no family?"

"Me? Oh, no. The fever took my Jimanez and the three children two years ago. I have been all alone since then. All I have left is Maria. I spoke to that donkey sheriff about her, and he says there is nothing he can do. She will say she chose to go with Ryan if he goes after her." She shook back the hair from her face. "She won't do that."

"There are some men here in town looking for me. I need to ride from here about midnight. I will check on her when I get down there. If I can, I will try to free her. You're sure she doesn't want to be with him?"

"Cross my heart." She handed him a bean burrito. "She does not love this man. What can I do about these men? The ones who look for you?"

Between bites of his spicy food, he shook his head. "Nothing. They won't find me."

"You no longer work for the Señora Peralta? Such a lovely woman."

"No, that was a short job." He smiled at her. "She is very pretty."

She wiped the tears from her face with a small cloth and tried to smile at him. "Then why did such a grand man as you leave her? She is a widow, no?"

"The same reason I must leave you at midnight. There are men looking for me."

She nodded in defeat.

"Your food is good." He held up what was left of the second tortilla. "You would spoil me."

"If I could. Get some sleep when you are ready. I will lay with you and you can hold me."

She went behind the divider to change, and came back in a nightshirt. "I will get you up by midnight."

He pulled off his other boot. "It is important that I get up and leave."

"Don't worry. I can do that."

Under the covers, she put her round butt against his belly

and clasped his hand to her right breast. He closed his leaded eyelids and fell asleep. Later, he awoke to her arousing him with her fingers jacking him off.

She rose under the covers and mischievously grinned out at him in the firelight. "I had to make him stiff."

He nodded and with his hands cradling her face, he brought her up and kissed her. "Francisca, you are a sweet person."

"You aren't mad? I mean, at me?"

"Never." He rose up so she could squirm beneath him. "Not ever."

On her back and looking up at him, she crossed herself. "Mother of God forgive me."

"She will. She will." He laughed as she wiggled to get it in place.

The cold stars were out watching him ride away. The declining moon rose when he was on the road headed south. He'd left her twenty-five dollars for firewood and food. In her case, a king's ransom. He'd also left a note to Perla that Francisca would be good help if Perla could use any more. And another she promised to post from him to Collie Bill, saying that Bledstone and their money had fled south and he was going after him.

The wind rose and it swirled brown dust in the air. Not as cold as in the mountains, but the stinging sand made him pull up his kerchief and closed down his vision. Several times, he used both hands to force his hat on tighter to keep from losing it. But a man who wore a felt hat all the time knew how to cock his head just enough so the wind never had much of chance to de-crown him.

He turned off the Taos Road and started for the San Juan Mission. Close to sundown, the light was fast retreating and he was tired of fighting the blustery wind. The waves of dirt were even obscuring his vision of the jacales that lined the road. Loose things rattled and cried as the wind tried to pry them loose. No one was outside in the bitter weather.

The LIVERY sign behind the veil of brown was welcome. Grateful for it, he dismounted and fought the door open. Inside, the hostler came and took his horse, promising to water and grain him. Satisfied, Slocum went out the walk-through doorway in the larger one and crossed to the cantina. Pressed by the wind, he soon was inside.

When he pulled down his kerchief, Casita, who was flirting with a man at the bar, saw him and rushed over. As if she trusted no one, she spoke in a soft voice. "What are you doing back here? I never thought I'd see you again."

"Where is Maria?"

Her dark eyelids narrowed looking up at him. "How do you know about her? Who told you?"

"Her sister Francisca asked me to see If I could help her."

"He would kill you. You can't go up there."

"Now listen, you tell me where she is and I'll find a way."

She closed her eyes and felt her forehead with her palm. "He has gunmen."

"Just tell me."

"There is a big brown house up the street on the right. But he has guards."

"I'll be back."

She clung onto his arm. "Oh, my darling, I will be so afraid for you. For your safety and everything."

"I'll be fine. Any of his men in here?"

She looked around, and then shook her head in strong disapproval. "Be careful. They are killers."

He left the cantina. The day was waning fast. He turned his back to the wind and checked the loads in his .44. If dust hadn't clogged it, he'd be fine. He saw the house and the low adobe yard wall she'd described to him. He went on the porch and knocked. Surprise sometimes gave one an advantage. Who'd expect him to be knocking?

The door opened and a sleepy-eyed guy looked out. "What ya want?"

Slocum slammed the door into him and clubbed him over the head in one fell swoop.

"Who is it?" Someone on the second floor shouted down from the head of the stairs. "It's you!" Ryan reached for his gun.

He already was in the blade sight of Slocum's .44. Slocum shot twice and the acrid gun smoke boiled up in the room. The candles went out and Slocum was in the dark downstairs.

Hard hit, Ryan pitched forward and came tumbling down the stairs—ass-over-teakettle until he sprawled on the last steps, his arms outstretched, and even in the poor light his blank eyes told Slocum enough. He bent over and jerked the gun out of the moaning guard's holster.

With a swift kick in the ass, Slocum minced no words. "The boss is dead. Get the hell out of town."

"I'm going. I'm going." He scrambled up, and went out the door on the run.

Slocum backed up and shut the door with his foot. Were there any more? All he could hear was the howling wind and the house creaking. He stuck the man's gun in his waistband and paused to reload his own. The cylinder clicking sounded loud enough to him as he turned it until an empty chamber was under the hammer.

His back to the wall, he began ascending the staircase—one step at a time. The six-gun in his fist was cocked and ready for anything. At the top, he stopped and listened. No sound gave away a thing. He'd have to search each room.

He went to the center room. The door was partially open. With the muzzle of the Colt, he pushed the door back and in the dim light, saw a naked girl sitting on the bed.

"Maria?"

She threw her head up and glanced at him. "It's you?"

"It's me." Then, as he came closer, he could see the chain from her wrist to the bedpost. "Does he have the key to those locks?"

"Yes."

"I ran one guy off. Is there anyone else in the house?"

She shook her head.

"I'll be right back. Don't cry. This is over. He's dead."

"I know—" She sobbed. "I—I just can't believe it."

25

Mary Murphy never even raised a dark eyebrow when Slocum stood behind the cardplayer opposite her. The bland look on her narrow face was cold as marble behind the fan of cards.

"Raise you twenty," she said, turning the ready chips in her other fingers.

"Hell, girl, you must have aces," the drawling Georgian said, and tipped his straw hat back on his head.

The last of the rich ones—if he was rich. Slocum had known several like him before the war. This dandy was unknown to him.

"I'll call you, darling."

She nodded and pressed three ladies on the table. "That good enough? I mean, for me to beat you."

He threw his hand up in the air. "You're mighty damn lucky at cards, little lady."

She raked in the pot, and then she put all of the stack in front of her in the drawstring purse. "You can come back to-morrow and try to win it back. You can't ever tell, *darling,* you might win it all back."

"I doubt that," Georgia said, laughing.

She joined Slocum at the bar, where he was sipping his whiskey. "Why send all that money to me? I don't understand," she said.

"Figured we'd need it."

"What for? You and me?"

"You and me are going to Tombstone, aren't we?"

She blinked up at him. "Sweet Jesus, you are serious? Aren't you?"

"I've got to find a man named Bledstone. He ran off with Collie Bill's and my reward money. Then we can go."

"I bet he's over at the Valhalla Bar. That's where he's been the last few nights playing cards."

"Let's go see before he loses all our money."

Bledstone had his broad back to the door when they slipped into the smoky bar. There was an empty chair across from him. Slocum took the seat and watched the man engrossed in counting his chips.

"I guess this game is open to all comers," Slocum said.

At the sight of him, Bledstone threw his head back in shock. "Slo—I thought—I mean I—"

"Gents, excuse us for a minute. He owes me a thousand dollars. I'm sure he can pay me. It's a little overdue."

Chairs legs scraped the floor and the other three players backed away. Slocum sat back in his chair and Mary moved in beside Bledstone. The flash of the nickel-plated derringer in her black-gloved palm with the muzzle pressed against his neck made the color drain from his face.

"I can't pay all of it—right now."

Slocum leaned forward. "How much do you have left?"

"Five-six hundred."

"Get it out and be real careful, her trigger finger is itchy."

"Yeah—yeah—" He began to frantically empty his pockets on the table.

Slocum reached across for the bills and began to straighten the crumpled ones and stack them in piles.

He cut Bledstone's talking off sharply. "Don't say another word. Keep digging."

At last, the money was counted. Mary slipped the small pistol in her purse and looked at Slocum.

"You're short three hundred and thirty-six dollars," he told Bledstone. "Where's your horse stabled?"

"You ain't taking my horse?" Bledstone whined.

Slocum leaned over the table. "Raise the rest by noon tomorrow and meet us back here, or I'll pull every damn gold tooth out of your head."

"I ain't got any gold teeth."

"I'll pull them till I find one."

Bledstone pushed away from the table. "You would, wouldn't you?"

Slocum nodded.

The passenger train rocked back and forth on the tracks headed west at twenty-five miles per hour. The smudged car windows were frosted, and the coal stove in the car was emitting some heat. New Mexico's desert took on many hues of tan and brown through the flurries of snowflakes outside. Under their wool blanket, the two of them snuggled to stay warm on their bench seat.

"Collie Bill has his money that you sent him. You have most of yours. Bledstone got real close," she said. "He only owes you forty-two bucks."

He flexed his stiff back. "I'll never see it."

"If you never see him again, that would be payment enough, right?"

"Exactly." And he kissed her. They'd be in Flag late that night, get a hotel room, and celebrate. Tombstone wasn't far away. Might stop over in Prescott and see the sights.

He hugged her under their cocoon. If he never saw that damn Bledstone again, it would be too soon.

Watch for

**SLOCUM AND THE RANCHER'S
DAUGHTER**

357th novel in the exciting SLOCUM
series from Jove

Coming in November!

APr. 2016